Brunella Longo

The Blind Spot
Adverse Childhood Experiences
And Autoimmune Diseases

Short stories

London
Online Data Assessment
2025

ISBN paperback: 978-1-8380909-9-9

Index

The burn

I feel a heat and hurry of the heart
That burns like joy
Swinburne (1)

Tuesday 5 September 2017

Two weeks until the next hospital appointment.

I want to ask questions.

How long do the consequences of a burn on a toddler's leg last? Does a burn injury jeopardise the development of a child? Does it have an impact on the immune system in later life? Do cells in the skin have a memory?

Did I really pedal the go-kart against the brazier? I wonder.

Does my childhood burn have any connection with my intolerance to smoke, or with the sense of suffocation that haunts me and holds me for hours after I smell barbecues, bonfires, or burning rubber? What about the allergy to smoked salmon that came out of the blue few years ago?

I want to speak with the doctors about these intolerances.

Questions like these have been spinning my mind since I last went to the clinic. They keep floating in front of me, fogging the visual field like there was something else I have to catch up with if I want to know where this disease comes from.

The aetiology of autoimmune diseases is fundamentally unknown, I read and read again, but this doesn't put my mind at rest. I am not convinced.

I do remember a certain aura of shame around the family tale of my burn, not only a medical concern. Why was that? There was a mist of religious beliefs, folklore, ideas of a spell put on me - that mist was the essence of Catholicism as it was practiced in the 1960s in the South of Italy.

Friday 8 September 2017

Since I've been waiting for a formal diagnosis, every day I surprise myself thinking about my disabled brother. I wonder why the influence he has had on the whole of my life continues to claim attention, even when it is clear I'd better think to my health.
Shall I indulge in these thoughts? Do they have any therapeutic purpose? Are they beneficial for mindfulness or anything else? I see I have such a peripatetic mind these days. It may be health anxiety or what they call 'brain fog'.
It seems just a bit weird. It is like waking up and meeting for breakfast with somebody who I know is actually almost dying and nonetheless smiles at me every morning, saying 'Hey, my princess. How are you today?"
I feel sucked into that blind spot, a place where the relationship I have with myself collapses into a greater dimension that is, perhaps, the relationship between the two of us. It's like my whole life has shrunk to the point of being only a small inner circle of living functions within the big Venn diagram of my disabled brother's life. And I would like to just speak with him, chat about our immense common nothingness, repeating the same words, and laugh, joking about the same sounds and shapes it seemed we were the only ones on earth able to notice along the road.
The world has changed, but in that blind spot we have remained the same, little kids with big differences. It still hurts.
I feel I need to breathe fresh air.

Saturday 9 September 2017

This is another kind of pain I have learnt to mitigate, to cope with or to deny by obfuscation - but it will never go away. Because I feel you are in my blood brother. Can you teach me something about my disease too?
My legs feel heavy, like I have been on a marathon. I can almost count my heartbeats if I pause and breathe and listen to the pulsations throbbing in my thighs, while I sit in front of the computer.
I think about you every day, although the time I could not imagine I would not care for you is long gone.

I remember a Sunday walk rambling down the mountains, the year before I left the Country. I suddenly felt I had to speak with your mother to say that I loved you both. I wonder why this tiny fragment of a short conversation of almost twenty years ago on a creepy telephone line keeps on bouncing back and forth in my mind, flickering in front of my blurred eyes, like a cherry pit spat out from a high-speed train window and instantly batted back in.

I do not know what was the reason why I felt that nervousness, the need to reassure mum. It may be a clue of something that happened to all of us, not just to me. There was undue pressure around us. I was left without any work. I was suddenly unwanted. And I could not care for you. I would not care for you. I will not care for you in the future. You will die and very likely I will not be with you.

This U-turn of destiny is still horrendous to think about at times.

Sunday 10 September 2017

We all had houses without heating. Not even fireplaces. There was just a simple, round brazier in the larger room of the house, usually a big kitchen and living room: a bowl shaped basin, in which coals and firewood logs would burn for few hours, mostly in the evening.

Around the brazier there was always a round footed clothes horse, and few stools. Nonna Maria Rosa and Nonna Grande Maria Stella were used to sit there. Other relatives, neighbours and friends would also sit down for a chat, coming and going.

The family's tale of the incident says that I was about three years old. I was riding a pedal go-kart when I bumped against the brazier, or perhaps it was the horse frame?

I might have been alone for a while. Perhaps the adults in the house were busy looking after my brother. For sure it was winter, as there was snow outside. I was wearing boots covering the ankles up to the lower legs.

A piece of ember, or a big spark of lighted coal?, must have hit the air around the brazier, and pirouetted down through the go-kart's cockpit straight into my left boot. The fragment of fire must have stayed stuck to the sock for an interminable moment.

It was like my joie de vivre had to pay a price in kind. The second degree burn two inches wide, just above the ankle joint, left a mark that is still very much visible 60 years on. The pain I must have endured for minutes, if not hours, even the smell of my flesh melting with the sock and the shoe, all these became details in my grandmother's tale of the brazier incident, recounted year after year.

When I look at it I see more than a scorch. It reminds me an entire ballast of feelings of sadness and sorrow that surrounded my enthusiasm for life until we moved far away, in another town in the North, after the legal separation of our parents.

Monday 11 September 2017

Sixty years on, it is like something in my blood, totally independent from my consciousness, reminds that there was a time in which I believed I was born to care for you, brother, even at such a young age. Father was used to say it was my destiny: you were born to get my care.

Our was a destiny of unity that forty years later your mother decided to destroy, choosing someone else as your power of attorney. Why? Why did I have to remove you from my life? Oh yes: I was unreasonably foolish about the future.

I imagined you would come and live with me. I would retire, and we would live by the sea. That was the true idea behind the flat I bought (and lost) in the South. That idea might have triggered the family's landslide against me. It was seen as a manifestation of insanity, a childish way to copy mum's pathological attachment to you, the buoyancy of a peri-menopausal spirit that does not really get where she comes from.

I wonder if you have ever understood the issue of mother's mind in a constant state of apprehensiveness about your future: at a certain point, it was like that anxiety mutated into a state of physical discomfort, produced mental confusion, built up lasting dysfunctions in the body. And became chronic. This might have been the way mother developed her autoimmune disease, the same way I am getting mine.

I think you knew. Perhaps not at all times, and not now, but I am sure you realised that. How many times I felt surprised by you saying you were sorry. It was clear we had to adjust behaviours, and make different plans, because of you. But you wanted to say sorry. Your empathy submerged us with tenderness, showing nuances of love and kindness inaccessible to us.

There was a time in which you and me would exchange a glance over the table and that was the only way to communicate while mother talked for you, upon you, on your behalf, about you. For how many years I tried to stop her from doing that? We would have liked to have that tacit conversation without her interference.

I wanted to listen to you when I came to visit. She wanted to control you in any way. Above all, I think she was fearing she could lose you, because of me. I could have taken over. Then you stopped glancing at me while she was talking: you surrendered to her will-power.

Things were changing for all of us in the 1990s. I was very busy, coming to see you only on Sundays, buying holiday packages for you and mum, sending postcards and presents from abroad. And then, there was no more way to secretly meet your mind just exchanging glances over the table. I wasn't able anymore to feel what you were feeling.

"Nel mezzo del cammin di nostra vita" I lost the ability to know what you were thinking, how you were feeling. Perhaps that was the moment I started to lose my destiny too, the core of my identity, the essence of being your sister, your princess. I wasn't mother's help anymore either. My role as your designated carer had already vanished, but I had not understood this. I did not really know what to say, what to do, where to go - without that destiny, and without my business.

What would become of me without a common future in old age? I did not have a husband, children, a family of my own because of a destiny that was now over.

Tuesday 12 September 2017

My autoimmunity issues might have started at that point. That would be consistent with many multidimensional definitions of the aetiology of autoimmune diseases I keep reading: experts agree that these conditions are triggered by a confluence of factors, many challenges at once the body and the mind are not able to cope with. It was like I was becoming deaf to myself, and to the rest of the world.

Let's try to focus on one thing at the time: I need to talk to the doctors about the burn. But what shall I say, how can I ask? It sounds bonkers. I don't have a direct memory of the incident, nor a medical record about the burn. Shall I just show the scorch? It is a bit laughable.

My own memory of the brazier incident had already faded away when I started to ask what was that strange medal of skin with different colour and texture on my leg. Everything else was changing size and shape in my body while I was growing up, but not the burn mark. How weird.

I remember both Nonna Maria Rosa and Nonna Grande Maria Stella repeating again and again how I risked my life. For several days I was unconscious, with high fever. Perhaps sepsi.

Something might have happened in my immune cells. Collagen, hormones, skin, all the organs must have screamed in horror. Perhaps, the whole body would remember that cellular scream forever.

The burn caused weeks of immense preoccupation for my health, I was told. There was no A&E or hospital in the village where we lived. Nonna Maria Rosa always mentioned the fact I had been very lucky because we had an important friendship with the only doctor living nearby, in the village. This doctor was rich, smart and proactive enough to put me on penicillin. Perhaps my toddler's body went into shock, with high sugar levels in my blood and a long-lasting infection, besides the fever?

Perhaps there were other complications nobody really understood? I do not know.

I remember only a vague image of Nonna Maria Rosa and Nonna Grande Maria Stella caring for me, in their long black dresses. Perhaps I lived with them while I was recovering, because my parents were too busy looking after my brother.

Wednesday 13 September 2017

Do you remember the Summer we went to see Frida, the movie? I think it was the last in which we spent some time together by the sea. You seemed so grateful that I took you to see that film. You sympathised with the story and the character since the first scene. We both discovered the life and work of the artist. You understood that you were not alone in feeling sad for what you could not do, for what we could not do for you, because there are indeed many people who are different, and live a life diminished by rare diseases, even without trisomy 21.

Thursday 14 September 2017

I had a look into clinical literature about the burn today although I did not go very far. I was distracted and nervous, as I am always when I know I am approaching something important that my mind is unprepared to hold.

Scientists want to experiment cell therapy for rapid tissue regeneration after burns. This is fascinating. There was something else to browse and learn about burns and autoimmunity but I lost myself into an article about experimental gene editing for the removal of the extra copy of chromosome 21 - that is what determines human trisomy 21, the abnormality that causes Down syndrome. The presence of an extra copy of this chromosome occurs in about one in seven or one in eight hundreds live births. Imagine a world in which the genetic defect of the extra chromosome is eliminated. How many lives could benefit from it! This fascinating breakthrough may be still far-fetched though. Gene editing innovations can be seen as morally unconceivable by some that do not see any defect at all in being born with an extra copy of chromosome 21.

Conversely, the idea of regeneration of skin tissue after burns is already endorsed by healthcare communities, and with several new products for skin tissue repairs authorised by the medical authorities in various Countries, it must be a really viable and uncontroversial option after life-changing injuries.

I may discover something else that explains a possible causative connection between burns in childhood and the development of autoimmune diseases later in life, if I do not get distracted.

Friday 15 September 2017

At least until the age of four, you were often vomiting without any reason. Your tongue was constantly out of your mouth. I remember this. The image I have in my mind must come straight from the heart, because there are no family photos showing you with that expression that still hurts me. It took mum a long, long time but she succeeded in teaching you how to keep your mouth close and with the tongue inside.

I do not know how she did it, but she made it. There was no medical advice on how she should or could treat you in those years. But it also took a long time for her to acknowledge that you had Down Syndrome, at the time still called mongolism (2): for many months either doctors refused to tell her clearly what was the cause of your health problems or she did not want to hear.

You travelled for days, months, years with mum and dad to visit doctors all around the Country, because mum was desperate to find a "cure". She wanted to know. There was nothing to know. I was waiting with Nonna Maria Rosa and Nonna Grande Maria Stella for you to come back from those trips: for us, you were the big boy doll of the house.

It sounds no surprise that I was just playing on my own, with your pedal go-kart, when I got the burn. It was because of you that dad had brought that avant-garde toy, a car. In the early 1960s only about one-third of households owned a car in Italy, and very likely, it was because of you that mum and dad decided to have one.

Those were years of fast social progress for some, sturdy resistance for others. Mum and dad ended up on two opposite slopes, and also that was because of you.

In the small village where we lived we were always together until I was 6 and you 5. I could not join the other children playing outdoor, barefoot, pretty much anytime of the year: you were unable to run, hide, jump. Occasionally, you stayed with Nonna Maria Rosa behind the counter of her grocery shop. Then, instead of just watching the other kids playing, I would join them in the street.

I have few visual memories of the two of us together in those days, around the time of primary school. And they stick like wax. We were inseparable until my Year 3, when you were neither accepted into nursery anymore (with me keeping an eye on you next door) nor you could enrol into normal Key Stage 1 classes.

Father drove us all towards a care home in the North of the Country, where he had been reassured you could receive special education. But it was untrue, and to get there he abandoned my small dog on the motorway, and dilapidated the savings Nonna Maria Rosa had given us to finish the building of a bigger family house.

I had weird episodes of urinary incontinence at school, after I saw how distressed you were in that "special education" institute. Mother's madness got us back to our unfinished house in the South. From then onwards she campaigned for pupils with special needs to

be accepted and educated in primary schools. Did you ever understand what all that mean to us, to me?
Your life has been so intertwined with all the choices we have made as a family and with everything that happened to all of us that I feel it is like we are all down, now that your body is falling in pieces brother. Old age brings sadness and health issues to everybody, but for you is being true hell.

Sunday 17 September 2017

Our parents had memories of my burn different from Nonna Maria Rosa's one. Their tale of the incident seemed to openly blame my tomboy character, and make fun of it. I might have risked my life playing unattended around the fire, but the burn mark was also testament to the insolence of a little girl who took over the pedal go-kart meant for her disabled brother.
I tend to exclude my brother could be able to push me, and the go-kart as well, towards the brazier. Did mum push me in a rage against me?

Monday 18 September 2017

Your spine was barely able to hold you upright. It took you another full year before you started to walk, while I was so precocious in everything.
The brazier incident was probably the first instance of a recurrent expression that mother would always find helpful to explain the cause of any of my problems: "it is because you wanted it". That phrase became the stamp of neglect deeply anchored in my heart. It was a lie, of course - because we were children. And she truly wanted me to unlearn dad's idea of a destiny upon us. But it was also stupid and even cruel.
Mum's lies were pouring from her own mental sufferance: she did not stop for a single day in her life to think what could have been of you, her beloved son, if you had not been disabled.
Her pride for your innumerable achievements (learning to read and write was extraordinary!) was coupled with despair for the Alzheimer's that quickly devoured your character, memory, and stamina after your 50th birthday. Yours were very much also mum's

and my achievements too in caring for you, in teaching you to ride the bicycle, the computer, how to ski, and to swim without aid.
You should have been intelligent, and brave: the son of your mother's pride, more than I was.
I had that insolence of playing with your pedal go-kart. But perhaps I was just entertaining you brother, I wanted to teach you how to pedal, I did not mean to steal your toy.

Tuesday 19 September

I went to look into the databases again today.
The "intricate cellular mechanisms of burn injury" and microvascular dysfunctions were the subject of a study published in 2016 in the "Journal of Burn Care & Research", a publication of the American Burn Association. I read that "thermal injury induces an immunosuppressed state that predisposes patients to sepsis and multiple organ failure" (3). Interesting to know.
The body of evidence is impressive: a burn can have impact in terms of cardiac stress, neurological, hepatic, pulmonary, gastrointestinal consequences, with renal failure occurring in up to 30% of patients with fire injuries.
Perhaps lymphatic memories of my burn reached my bones and settled into the surrounding soft tissue?   at that young age, was the burn a trauma for the bone marrow, the "factory" of our immune cells?
Scientists have recently found evidence that the lymphatic system extends much wider than previously thought: lymphatic vessels exist even in bones (4).
Damaged skin tissues and vessels after a burn can trigger a "systemic inflammatory response syndrome" that may alter the development of the immune system.
Experts say that "severe burns induce response that affects almost every organ system. Inflammation, hyper-metabolism, muscle wasting, and insulin resistance are all hallmarks of the pathophysiological response to severe burns, with changes in metabolism known to remain for several years following injury". On top of that "burns not only destroy the barrier function of the skin but also alter the perceptions of pain, temperature and touch".

These are terrific scientific news. Associations between fire injuries and autoimmunity problems are not just an idea of mine. Eventually, an answer to my question, at least a potential one, is emerging.

I have more confidence to bring such questions to my next hospital appointment.

I remember one of the few conversations I had with my late father: "you could have asked for more, did you ask for more?" he repeated several times the same adagio referring to total different contexts. Now I feel I understand what he meant, albeit he seemed really confused. Neither dad had an easy healthy life, away from us. He needed to find himself too, at a distance from mum's obsession with Down syndrome, and I do not know if he ever found some peace. I never blamed him for leaving us. He married again, and forgot us for about two decades, as we forgot him. He had other children, we had another destiny.

Everybody coming to visit us had eyes only for you: all the adults seemed convinced that my destiny of neglect was acceptable, inevitable, normal. I knew that everybody loved me but it was another kind of love.

I was the child that had a chance to make our parents happy before you were born. For such a short time I was loved immensely. I saw it in the pictures. But that lasted only 16 months. Then, and for many years afterwards, our parents' only reason to live seemed to be seeking a "solution" to the problems you unexpectedly brought into the family.

They had planned to enjoy the early 1960s Italian economic boom, not to be consumed by the medical ignorance and social hostility towards people with Down syndrome and their families.

After the legal separation, mum specialised as a primary teacher for pupils with special needs. The hardship of our daily life remained entirely on her shoulders. She fought and won many battles to make you able to read and write, have basic numeracy skills, be able to socialise.

My emotional development and wellbeing become even more complicated, patchy, self-taught, in the shade of mum's overarching mission: I became who I am only because of a great love for life, growing up in the pauses from my main role in the house. I read all the books about everything that I found at school or in the public library until I realised I couldn't be mother's help forever. I had to find a job, and my independence away from you. And she did not want me to be around after all.

Wednesday 20 September 2017

The doctor confirmed the diagnosis of autoimmune disease. I knew. I was prepared. Nonna Maria Rosa had one, my mother had another one. All the clues were there.

I do not feel anything today, only thirst. I am very tired. I keep on thinking it is not cancer. However, autoimmunity is extremely unlikely to go away once it sets in. It explains why my quality of life has been deteriorating so much after the menopause. I need to check regularly that it remains in a stable condition as much as possible, and it does not turn into cancer.

Nobody really knows why some people get these diseases - the doctor cut shortly. Autoimmune diseases develop in people with several genes' mutations (or none) who have been exposed to environmental, immunological, neurological and lifestyle factors.

Like burns in childhood? Like loosing one's destiny? I would have liked to ask.

I wanted to put forward my hypothesis and doubts but there was no time for questions or conversations about my burn and other adverse childhood experiences. The reason of my susceptibility to autoimmunity remains a mystery.

I came home wondering if other siblings of people with Down Syndrome tend to develop autoimmune diseases. Wouldn't it be quite interesting to see if this question has any statistical significance in a genome-wide association study?

Thursday 21 September 2017

Mother would possibly shout at me 'don't say silly things'. Being the mother who has been caring for a Down syndrome son for more than sixty years, she can say whatever she wants, and still be utterly credible. With a high degree of confidence, she could even say that playing with your go-kart as a tomboy toddler was the sin that triggered my disease, a lifelong punishment for my untamed, buoyant attitude of querying, poking, challenging my destiny. It happened because I wanted it.

My symptoms are just a pale echo of yours. At your age, people with Down syndrome very likely develop several autoimmune diseases on top of muscular hypotonia, laxity in the joints, neuro-sensorial defects, the early-onset of Alzheimer's, celiac disease and more.

My mind sways towards the differences that always existed between us, that are not just in the number of chromosomes. You got all your teeth replaced by implants by the age of 30. I struggled to find the money to pay for my three. You had a cornea transplant to prevent risks of blindness because of keratoconus - and I am not sure I would have consented to, if somebody had asked me (perhaps it is just a coincidence, but your speech and mental agility started to deteriorate after the cornea transplant). Conversely, I waited years to have appointments with rheumatologists and other specialists and for a diagnosis. And so on and so forth.

It is because I wanted all this to happen? Anyhow, it does not matter what mum would say now. I remember when we were used to look into each other's eyes, brother, and exchange those meaningful glimpses about the truth.

Notes

(1) Swinburne, AC., *Bothwell: A Tragedy*, 3rd ed, London, Chatto and Windus, 1874.

(2) The condition, attributed to the chromosomal anomaly trisomy 21 in 1959, was then named after John Langdon Down who described it for the first time in 1866 as a "Mongolian type of idiocy". The term mongolism in scientific literature was dropped only between 1964 and 1966, at first by "The Lancet", then by the World Health Organisation, following complaints by scientists and parents increasingly embarrassed and offended. People with Down syndrome were found in all ethnic groups. However, still in the 1970s was very frequent that not only popular press but even teachers and healthcare professionals continued to use the word 'mongolism', the sharp decline of which coincided in the 1990s with the introduction all over the world of blood test screenings for an early detection of the condition during pregnancy. In the 1990s, campaigns by parents associations promoted the adoption of new social care policies that led

to the so called "deinstitutionalisation" in several Western Countries: this brought to an end the practice of leaving children with Down syndrome in long-stay mental hospitals where they would be forgotten, experience violence and trauma, unlikely to survive the age of 30. A Down syndrome Association was set up in the UK in 1970. The Italian equivalent was established only in 1988, although regional and provincial groups of parents were active since the 1970s. The European Down syndrome Association (EDSA.EU) was established in 1987. The first clinical guidelines for the medical care of adults with Down syndrome, the life expectancy of whom now extends over 60, were published only in 2020, under the considerable influence of the Global Down Syndrome Foundation, established as a non profit organisation in the United States in 2009.

(3) Colton B. Nielson et al, *Burns: Pathophysiology of Systemic Complications and Current Management*, J Burn Care Res; 2017, 38:e469–e481.

(4) Schwaerzer, G., *Lymphatic vessels identified in bones*, Nature cardiovascular research 2023, 2, 223.

Schirmer's test for a man

"Can I have your name?"

"Sam Wilkinson"

"Date of birth?"

"Fourth of July Nineteen Seventy Three"

"And how are you today Mr Wilkinson?"

"Ugh. It looks I am having a flare… inflammation, pain everywhere… you know… perhaps an ongoing infection, Sjögren's life (1)… just when I was about to go on holiday… it's not fair, is it?". He's fishing for pity from the nurse.

"Oh, I am sorry to hear Mr Wilkinson", she promptly comments. "Unfortunately dry eyes get easily infected either with viruses or bacteria. Do you always use warm compresses and do your eye bath? you use the artificial tears regularly?"

She looks at the computer screen, typing into online forms, inputting data from the rheumatologist's manuscript note he handed to her after the consultation.

Sam knows the protocol. They have lot of admin work to do for these minimal routine examinations: first the eyes, then the blood tests, etcetera. Every few years they repeat check-ups that do not actually add, explain, subtract anything to his disease management. But that's the way it goes.

"Oh yes", he lies. "Compresses twice or three times a day, eye drops just twice a day if I am lucky but most days up to ten times, you know…".

"Good for you, Mr Wilkinson!". The nurse's tone says she's perfectly aware that compliance with the eyelids warm compresses by patients with KCS or DED (2) is utterly complicated, and generally very poor. On top of that, the eye drops may disturb vision in the long run. There isn't much else patients can do to ease the grittiness of meibomian gland dysfunction and dry eye diseases. The clinical evidence and the range of products on the market put forward by pharmaceutical companies is hugely in favour of using and abusing of these liquid viscous eye drops that may increase intra-ocular pressure, and they may have a range of other side effects. Not to mention the punctal plugs (3), an idea he very much associates with research done in nazi concentration camps.

"Well, it would be better if I swayed in a Caribbean hammock, between trees, facing a beautiful sandy beach… would you come to test me there?". He hasn't lost the people pleaser attitude of his youth, nor the occasional skirt chaser, when not comic womaniser wit. When he feels anxious, and the lack of saliva does not compromise his willingness to chat, he can still be very talkative, even enticing. Tentatively. He knows he often ends up looking and feeling somehow pathetic these days, but it is a personality trait of his, not just a habit, and that hasn't completely changed after the disease, reassuring him he still has his own identity: it is a comfort for him to remember that for a long time he had a reputation of being a funny lad among friends and colleagues, and a handsome guy female friends found quite exciting to have around. Everybody wanted him at parties or dinners because of his jokes. Things change in life, but he is still Sam.

"No problem Mr Wilkinson" the nurse replies, not impressed. "This will not take long and then you are free to go and enjoy the summer weather". She shows compassionate professionalism to her best, after all.

Sam stares at the nurse's dress neckline under the gown, while she puts on a pair of latex-free gloves. Perhaps she should lose a couple of stones, she is clearly overweight, he reckons.

The nurse wheels her chair away from the desk and the computer screen, reaching the drawers on her side. She grabs the strips.

"Thank you" he replies, serious.

Sam sits back, reclining the chair, lays his neck on the pillow, slides the elbows on the armrests, in silence. He has good manners too, and it is time to calm down, to relax his spine and shoulders against the faux-leather, still lukewarm after the previous patient.

"You know what this test is for? Why the rheumatologist sent you to the eye clinic, Mr Wilkinson?". The nurse asks protocol's questions.

Evidently she does not have full access to his medical record, he believes, that it's not a bad thing after all the cyber attacks to hospitals happened in recent times.

Sam feels the sting of something irritating his throat that lasts few seconds and narrows his airflows. It must be the air conditioning system. It could end up with a coughing attack, or an impossible to manage urgency to spit: it would not be easy to handle in this situation. The last time it happened he was in a similar situation at the dental clinic where he avoided suffocation spitting violently on the floor, with a nurse jumping back, the cleaner called in, another nurse sent in to help but there was anything to help: the attack lasted literally few seconds. Nothing he had not talked about in previous occasions.

He deeply breathes in and out through the nose, recruiting all the saliva he can swallow down, so that he can avoid coughing or choking.

"It's because of my Sjögren's annual check-up" he eventually replies, back in control of his irritated larynx.

He has been quizzed again and again with the same identical questions for over a decade. Eventually, he learned to talk about his disease robotically: there is no need to put effort in such "how much sick you are" conversations that perpetuate a sensation of helplessness. Like most of social media posts he still tries to read with sincere attention from time to time, chatting about his condition leaves him very tired. The whole humanity is busy, he's left behind.

Sometimes he just collapses into that feeling his dad would call sadness. Regrettable. He knows the right word for it: hopelessness. Sorting out a symptom, just to make space for another one to show up the day after, and then another one, and then another one: this is, at its core, disease management in Sjögren's. He's become a champion of tactics for it.

"Oh yes, things change at all times, Mr Wilkinson, especially as we age", the nurse comments. She too has a sort of scripted way to interact with patients. Years ago he would have found it quite irritating, as he was still trying to have real, open-hearted conversations with medics and paramedics. Now he does not bother anymore. The risk of rage, and then more stress, is always over the corner at the hospital, like the risk of more infections. They should just stop everything in healthcare and rebuild the national health system from scratch, this is what he often thinks when he comes for the check-up.

"Schirmer's test measures how dry are your eyes. Now I am going to put these two tiny paper strips on your lids margins, Mr Wilkinson. You please look up for me, no no, not to the left, straight up please. Try not to move your head. Look up up up". She leans towards him.

"Alright". He just has to do this. He would like to turn silent and relax but a certain degree of nervousness takes over and makes him talk again quickly: something inside would like to delay this procedure, or cancel it altogether, and just go home and make a cup of tea.

So he ends up moving his wrists nervously on the armrests, in an attempt to distract the nurse from going on doing what she has to do: "Do you practice other tests here, or just Schirmer's?" he asks, with a foolish, hoarse voice.

The nurse does not talk. Instead she calmly and firmly place the palm of her left hand flat on his forehead while she hooks one of the two strips to his right bottom eyelid. Then she quickly repeats the gesture, putting the other strip into his left eyelid.

Eventually she answers: "Here? We do all the dry eye tests, Mr Wilkinson". She quickly, and robotically adds that yes, in this clinic they perform many tests for all sorts of diseases of the eyes but this is the only one he was required to do for today.

She may not like chatting with patients, Sam notes to himself, so she retracts into robotic conversations.

"A couple of minutes and it will be all done, Mr Wilkinson. I can see already you have very little tears to wet the strip. Try to relax, you can blink normally or keep your eyes closed, but please do not move your head too much. Yes, yes, keep your eyes closed if it helps. Where are you going on holiday, Mr Wilkinson?".

"I am visiting relatives, they live in the South of France, Marseille, have you been there?".

"No, I have never been there, Mr Wilkinson. Are you from France?".

"My mother. I was born in England but we lived there until I was 9 years old because of my father deployment to the South of France. He was in the Royal Navy. They were used to have joint operations with the French naval task force there."

"Oh I see".

"It's almost unthinkable that I suffer from lack of tears". He continues, keeping his eyes closed as this minimises the irritation caused by the paper strips.

"As a child I was prone to cry at all times" he continues "I was able to do so for an interminable time, to the despair of my mother who went on for years shouting at my tantrums: Sam, stop it. You have a crying disease!".

"Oh I am sorry to hear that Mr Wilkinson. Why was that?" The nurse sounds genuinely, empathically interested.

"I do not really know. My father would just repeat quietly, without losing his temper, that boys do not cry, you know.... But my mother comment would always be... how can I say? well, raw, even cruel. She would shout things like Leave him alone, he has the crying disease... She was always busy, nervous, you know... mother of three boys... Probably she already had some autoimmune disease herself to complicate her life even further. I was always getting hugs from granny, and words of consolation from dad. But my mother did not like the idea I could cry, with no reason. Or maybe I had a reason, but nobody understood it".

"What do you think, Mr Wilkinson? Did you have a reason for those tantrums?", she asks.

He feels the friction of the strips against the eyelids.

"I cannot remember any", he actually lies.

He wants to end this little torture of the unnecessary Schirmer's test as soon as possible now and go out in the sunshine, with his hat and glasses, without transforming this procedure in a mock of a psychotherapeutic session.

Sam perfectly remembers how darkness caused him to burst into tears easily: crying was a solution, to release tension. His dad put some fairy lights yellow red and blue in his bedroom, in granny's bedroom and along the corridor too.

The faux-leather of the nurse chair makes a squeal. She repeats they have now to wait just a few minutes to see how much he's going to wet the strips for the test.

Mentioning Marseille has pulled out from his family memories, often locked away from him and his daily routines, a vague but coloured visual memory of a quarrel about something, after which his mother locked him in the darkness of granny's bedroom. It was very dark indeed. He remembers the smell of the sea lavender coming in from outside the house, as a comfort. Why did she want to give him that cruel punishment, and for several years?

He heard mother saying once that granny was used to lock her away in the basement, without lights, so it must have been a sort of family imprinting… she must have thought that inflicting that punishment on him was part of an obvious style of parenting.

Now that he suffers from absence of tears, even when he would really like to cry, he wonders whether the lack of lachrymal fluid, his partially evaporative dry eye disease, has anything to do with that darkness punishment, with the torments his mother suffered for many years, projecting on him her depression.

As a child, he was often overwhelmed with emotions he could not understand. Feelings that scared him to death, like the ones caused by darkness, haunted and held him for hours or even days.

He was an enthusiast child, eager to learn from the world of busy adults. But left alone he could often be sucked into that strange inner place of unexplained suffering. He cannot say why. At a certain moment, the frustration inside and around him would push him in that emotional cul-de-sac. The only way out was an outburst of unconsolable, but liberating, crying.

Later on, entering his teens, he became slowly aware of what his father meant. Crying was not seen as a normal thing to do for a man. Grown up boys do not cry: if they do, the crying tantrum does not really ease the pressure of intense emotions. On the contrary, the tears could add something else even more difficult to explain to others: teachers and classmates would start asking questions. He would not be able to talk through. Some would judge he was an easy prey for bullies - in particular, he remembers a certain girl he tried to kiss once - and the whole thing turned out just utterly unbearable, impossible to justify, too much to cope with.

There was nobody he could trust capable of understanding his irresistible instinct to cry for nothing. And so he just stopped crying: he made it by way of imposing something else on his mind to think about and handle. He started laughing instead, often inventing stories that would distract him and others from any potential emotional hijacking.

Instead of crying his undecipherable heart out, he found there was another great way to release tension: making jokes, being funny, be the acting buffoon of his class and, later on, at work too.

He reckons now, at 59 years of age, that he must have had terrible feelings of inadequacy and guilt to process as a child, and later as a teenager. But now... is another life, another world.

"So have you been suffering from dry eye since long, Mr Wilkinson?", the nurse's breath lands on him again. He opens his eyes, and sees her leaning over his forehead.

The big breasts of the nurse are almost touching his chin, so that he is tempted to say something fun, and wrong, once again. She removes the strips.

He was not expecting to remember his fear of darkness, and childhood tantrums. The sad confirmation of dry eyes, on top of his dysfunctional meibomian glands (4), is what he was expecting today, but... You never know what happens with these trips to the hospital.

The nurse says the strips have retained very little wet. Yes, not a surprise, he comments.

"Ten years now" he says, almost whispering, like he's talking to himself, making the count. Then he look at the nurse in the eyes. He would like to be funny but... He restrains himself this time.

"My mother went on saying bitterly that I had that crying disease", he just says again, but this time he does it in a sarcastic tone, almost to counterbalance the previous emotional intimacy moment. He found unbelievable at first to be given the diagnosis of an autoimmune disease that disproportionately affects women, more than men, in the ratio of nine out of ten.

"What a mother's prophecy., Mr Wilkinsons". The nurse is smiling, eventually. They are on the same wavelength now, denying uncomfortable yet medically insignificant truths.

Now that he does not cry anymore to release a state of deep, profound emotional or moral sufferance, it looks like his immune system has just revolted against him.

As a child, he believed his mother's words: that he had a crying disease, that it was like flu or cough, but with no cure, and that was what it made him crying for nothing.

Today he would rather have the crying disease than Sjögren's!

"I know I know, Mr Wilkinson", the nurse is saying, while she puts his Schirmer's strips, the rheumatologist's manuscript note and some other printouts in a transparent plastic pocket. She then sticks a label on it and put it in a basket on the shelf behind her desk.

"As we grow up we loose that natural way to express emotions, Mr Wilkinson. It happens to everybody. Sometimes, also positive emotions can have a strong impact on a child".

He understands she must be thinking to something personal. He detects she has an East-European accent, and perhaps a hint of nostalgia in her voice. Has she left someone behind in her Country? Visual memories of the former Yugoslavia wars of the 1990s, when he was still working in a busy newsroom, come along, filling him with empathy, and a sort of incomprehensible remorse.

"Yes, you're right" he says.

Sam consciously tries to return to his present day of dryness.

"I totally lost my way to the tears", he says, before smiling to the nurse: "Thank you, you have a nice day".

I just lost the tears, he repeats to himself heading towards the lift.

He hasn't lost himself in dark places though!

There is nothing really funny about his life these days, but he laughs all the same.

NOTES

(1) Sjögren's typical clinical feature, associated with arthralgia (joints pain, like in arthritis and other rheumatic conditions), is keratoconjunctivitis sicca (KCS). KCS affects the conjunctiva, the cornea and the eyelids. In Sjögren's, KCS is due to an aberrant, autoimmune infiltration of some immune cells into the lacrimal, the salivary and other exocrine glands that causes dryness of mucosal membranes in the whole body. Sjögren's is often evident mainly in the eyes and in the mouth, because of the gritty eyes and the lack of saliva, at least at the initial stages of the disease. To mitigate the symptoms patients need to prevent flareups of inflammation and infections, avoiding dust, smoke, excess of heat and cold temperature that would make easier for the immune system to overreact or, on the contrary, to be too slow and too weak to fight infections. Using artificial tears during the day and eyes ointments at bedtime gives temporary relief, although there may be consequences for the wellbeing of the eyes in the long run. Many other little remedies help to mitigate the dry eyes problem, in particular acting on the meibomian glands in the eyelids: hydration, constant balanced body

temperature, not eating anything spicy, wearing photo-reactive spectacles and hats to protect the eyes from intense light and glares at all times, fighting any sign of infections very timely are the most common remedies.

(2) KCS is often considered synonym of Sjögren's, being the most common and evident sign of this autoimmune disease. But the term can also be used to refer to a severe stage of dry eye disease (DED), in which similar symptoms occur without involvement of immune cells. When KCS occurs, independently from its complex aetiology and manifestations - viral, toxicological, bacterial, toxic, injuries or autoimmune - it is good clinical practice that patients are tested for objective measurements, like Schirmer's test and the presence of typical antibodies recurrently found in the blood of patients with the condition. All the available clinical guidelines for the assessment and the effective management of KCS so far (2025) recommend a comprehensive approach to the disease that is recognised to be part of an abnormal "inflammatory cascade and immune response". For a synthetic but thorough overview about KCS and all its clinical and diagnostic tests, including lab tests for specific aetiologies see: Burrow, MK et al, *Keratoconjunctivitis*, StatPearls [Internet]. Last update February 6, 2025.

(3) Many diagnosed with Sjögren's disease are offered punctal plugs. Rheumatologists and ophthalmologists consider them one of the default treatments for dry eyes disease. Punctal plugs emerged in the 1960s as an alternative to the permanent chemical cautery occlusion of the puncta, practiced since the late 1930s. Like minuscule bathtub drain stoppers, punctal plugs are made of silicone rubber or other polymer and are inserted in the tear duct of the eye to ensure tear conservation. At least, this is the theory. In 2017 a Cochrane review provided evidence that punctal plugs can exacerbate the problem of dry eyes and related pathologies, from chronic conjunctivitis to recurrent infections. My own opinion is that the method ignores the role of the lymphatic system in the body, of the eye immune system and the immune cells in the tissue surrounding the eyes, and the tear duct. With Sjögren's and other autoimmune diseases the lymphatic system needs extra care and stimuli to function in spite of its impairment, and not to be impaired even further. See: Ervin AM, Law A, Pucker AD, *Punctal occlusion for dry eye syndrome,* Cochrane Database of Systematic Reviews 2017, Issue 6.

(4) MGD stands for meibomian gland disfunction. Together with inflammation of the conjunctiva and blepharitis (very often due to demodex infection) MGD is a very common complication in Sjögren's, occurring in 20 up to 80% of patients according to various studies: facilitated by the evaporation of tears, by cell debris and by the hardening of the oily layer in their terminal ducts, these tiny glands get easily blocked. The impaired or obstructed secretion of their special lipid secretion, in turn, affects the quality of the tear film perpetuating the dryness even when the eye is lubricated with artificial tears, with risks that the irritated ocular surface creates corneal staining. Treatments offered by private clinics in recent years for dry eye disease and MGD are technology based and consists of Intense pulsed light (IPL) or the application of mechanical / termal pressure to the eyelids (Lipiflow). Over a thousand studies and registered clinical trials have been assessed and reviewed to conclude these treatments haven't produced sufficient, uncontroversial evidence of effectiveness compared to more traditional care methods, such as warm compresses and lubrication. See Cote, S. et al, *Intense pulsed light (IPL) therapy for the treatment of meibomian glands dysfunction*, Cochrane Database of Systematic Reviews Review, 18 March 2020. In the UK, NICE, the National Institute for Care Excellence, published a Medtech innovation briefing document (*LipiFlow thermal pulsation treatment for dry eyes caused by blocked meibomian glands*, Medtech innovation briefing n. 29, 21 April 2015). Finally, a systematic review published in 2025 concluded that "the current clinical trial evidence regarding the comparative effectiveness and safety of LipiFlow for treating meibomian gland dysfunction (MGD) and dry eye disease (DED) of other etiologies is limited and inconclusive". See: Pucker AD, Yim TW, Rueff E, Ngo W, Tichenor AA, Conto JE. *LipiFlow for the treatment of dry eye disease*, Cochrane Database of Systematic Reviews 2024, Issue 2. Although the scientific evidence is low, several clinics now offer these technology based treatments.

The Blind Spot

Over a period of more than thirty years Simon Legdemund was diagnosed with a variety of diseases due to an overactive, intolerant, dysfunctional immune system: juvenile arthritis, rheumatoid arthritis, inflammatory bowel disease, Crohn's disease, ulcerative colitis, ankylosing spondylitis and more. Until a young rheumatologist told him he actually had "only" Sjögren's disease (1).

That should not surprise him, the specialist said: even if it seemed dismissive to hear, fact is that Sjögren's progresses slowly over decades, mimicking disturbances typical of many non specific diseases (like bronchitis or cystitis) as well as immune disorders (like vasculitis or Lupus, for instance).

The awkward, subtle nature of the condition explains the kaleidoscope of symptoms, often mild, sometimes severe, that patients may experience over a long period of time.

Simon was not surprised at all: his health had already been a whack-a-mole game for ages so that whatever new diagnosis of an additional or a different autoimmune disease without a definitive cure would not make much of a difference to him anymore. At 62 years of age the only thing that really mattered to him was to keep any pain in the body at bay, sleep well and enjoy himself as much as possible - that was a really tricky task to accomplish every day.

The rheumatologist was relieved to see him in good spirit. However he was also very sorry that there weren't convenient systemic medications to prescribe in Simon's case, because he had experienced severe side effects to several drugs generally well tolerated by people with rheumatoid arthritis, Lupus or the same Sjögren's and even a couple of almost allergic (anaphylactic) reactions.

"At any rate, Mr Legdemund, Simon if I may, you are doing very well. Sometimes, the best line of action with Sjögren's, at least up to a certain severity of symptoms, is... inaction. Do nothing, wait and see, distract yourself, be monitored in any case with annual check-ups to make sure you do not develop malignancies, and make sure you react promptly with diet and lifestyle and talking with your GP if you see unexpected changes... Always stay away from anything that creates stress or food intolerances. I am sure you will be alright and I'll see you in a year time".

At the end of the consultation, Simon felt he had something to get off his chest before leaving: his social life was shrinking, causing him great sadness and solitude, he said, on top of the numerous limitations and impairments caused by his autoimmunity. He had opted for an early retirement option to work as a part-time bookkeeper during the pandemic, family did not see him anymore as a good fit for parties or reunions, because of his obsession with opening the windows to have more ventilation, wiping with antiseptic everything, eating his own lunch boxes and the like. Friends and neighbours seemed at times fading away too, because he did not drink anything other than water, going to the pub would be a little torture for him with people normally drinking alcohol, and smoking or vaping outside, beside the fact he did not eat red meat, nor fries, anymore but very occasionally. "It's quite a lonely existence having this whack-a-mole disease, no matter the name".

"Ha. perhaps there is something that may be interesting for you" the rheumatologist was happy to advice, at last: "there is a group of colleagues currently recruiting participants for a new research programme. It does not require you to take any medication, it is not a clinical trial for new drugs, but it would put you in contact with a group of other people having a mix of conditions, with situations similar to yours, multiple diagnosis over time, no response to medications and the like. Shall I gave your name? Half of the participants needs to have some kind of psychiatric illness, that is not your case, while the other half needs to have been recently diagnosed with Sjögren's. Shall I pass your details Simon? what do you think? It could be an opportunity for you to discuss your medical history, get access to some relevant, recent scientific discoveries, know other patients, socialise more...".

"By all means" Simon said straightaway. The idea was absolutely fine with him, although he had refused for a long time to liaise with other ill, disabled or troubled people. But this time around it seemed that the purpose of the initiative could overshadow social aspects he would otherwise find depressive. He had spent years reading books and clinical guidelines and research papers about his complex disease. It would have been fantastic to have the opportunity to hear others' views and experiences in a collaborative study. The rheumatologist promised to recommend Simon to his colleagues: he was sure the leader investigator, Dr Brian Gee, would be very interested in having him on board.

Brian Gee was actually on a mission, Simon noticed after few minutes he started talking about "The Blind Spot" programme at their first, introductory meeting.

"In spite of considerable interest from the scientific and the clinical practice communities,   and several observational studies, no consistent reliable evidence has emerged so far about the causal link between autoimmune diseases and schizophrenia spectrum disorder" Gee said, explaining that his research team had identified data from GWAS (genome wide association studies) that seemed to demonstrate there was a common autoimmune origin between schizophrenia spectrum disorder and several autoimmune diseases (2).   Thus, the purpose of the programme was to collect more qualitative and quantitative information that would contribute to clarify such association.

All the other 19 participants were women, with the exception of only another middle age man, Sam Wilkinson, a nice guy.

The study wanted to investigate the association between development, personality traits and early signs of immune dysfunctions and / or psychiatric illnesses, for which the participants would be asked to provide a large amount of personal data through questionnaires, diaries of symptoms, logs recording foods consumed, medications and activities. Also their structured and unstructured exchanges of views, childhood memories, interactions and discussions, browsing history and other technical data would be taken into account by the research team and analysed through AI software.

The programme was meant to last ten months, with monthly meetings of three hours each, plus a series of activities everybody could do in their own time from home, reporting back online through an online platform.

They could also have video calls and chats online as much as they liked, exchange information and advice, and doing whatever they wanted but beware everything would be on record, and although with a very high level of privacy protections there was no 100% guarantee against cybercrime or other risks of oversharing so be mindful that there might be convenient a certain level of redaction.

There is a video tutorial on the platform advising on how to redact personal information and not oversharing data during the programme: they should feel free to watch it and if they needed more help he and other members of the team would be always welcoming whatever question and comment they may have.

Brian Gee asked if everybody agreed to proceed with their own brief introduction, saying what they had been diagnosed with, if they wished so.

A slim lady with a beautiful smile but for very swollen cheeks and neck (probably a goitre, Simon thought) asked if they would be required to take any medication for the purpose of the study. No, Brian patiently reiterated this was not a clinical trial in any possible way. Instead the research programme could be considered an exploration of the potential of patients engagement in the creation of collaborative knowledge. The study would analyse their shared lived experience of different autoimmune and neurological diseases, plus the team and the same participants' observations. However, if they wanted to provide feedback or notes about their medications they could do it online: any information would be always looked into and appreciated.

Another lady said she had various conditions, including multiple sclerosis. She explained there was a time in which she thought she would start studying immunology, after her first rheumatologist insisted saying she had a self-destructive disease. She found that way to talk to her very upsetting, utterly depressing: she did not believe at all she was a self-destructive person. Brian Gee, who was himself an immunologist, found absolutely pertinent to say something about his discipline. Quoting Paul Ehrlich, who had coined the term "horror autotoxicus" to turn down the idea of autoimmunity as unthinkable, Gee explained that after many years of intellectual, almost religious, rejection of that blasphemous hypothesis, scientists found that the "horror autotoxicus" was actually very true: in the 1950 and 1960 the discovery of antibodies, biomarkers found in the blood of patients with autoimmune diseases, showed patterns of symptoms typical of certain conditions and not others. This led to the wide acceptance of the theory of "self" versus "non self" in immunology, still very much endorsed by many scientists and organisations today. However, there is also a growing body of evidence suggesting this self and non-self distinction does not explain how the immune system works in health and disease, although it may remain a valid simplification for educational purposes. In sum, the immune system can either show some defects at birth or lose its way to distinguish between foreign intruders (pathogens) and its own cells during childhood and in other critical life periods but, as the team hopes to do with "The Blind Spot" programme, there is more, much more, to understand in autoimmune diseases. In particular, there is certainty of an individual unique mixture of genetic and environmental factors, the coalescence of which determines that sort of blind spot in the regulation of the immune system: each of us has a network of cells, tissues and ducts capable of self-damage, a place in which the immune system loses its ability to self-regulate and starts damaging the body instead of protecting it.

There were any questions, so after that round of presentations, and few jokes about who was self and who was non-self, the participants went straight into the first activity of the day.

The exercises they would always be asked to do, in person or online, required writing down answers to broad questions or reactions to statements about diseases and their aetiology. They did not have to put their name if they preferred to remain anonymous, neither they had to necessarily share and discuss their answers, Brian clarified once more. The first of these exercises required to answer the question: "*Explain if you have experienced something that relies to the notion of "blind spot" in your immune system, when or why do you believe something went wrong in the ability of your immune system to regulate itself, independently from any event, actual disease or diagnosis you experienced in the aftermath of it.*"

Gee invited everybody to take their time. If in 15 minutes they did not come up with anything they should not worry or panicking, as they could always do or repeat the exercise at a later time on the online platform. Also, there was no obligation to read aloud and share with others what they put down, but anything they said would be recorded and available to the research team at large.

After the 15 minutes time expired, the youngest woman in the group, with a big pair of fancy glasses, volunteered to start sharing what she had written down: 29 years old, she was diagnosed with attention deficit and disruptive behaviour disorder at the age of 13, then she had varicella (chickenpox) and a diagnosis of autism. Medics completely ruined her education, she said. Years later, she was diagnosed with Type 1 diabetes. Everything in her life changed again, but for the better. She is okay now with lot of helping technologies to manage the condition. However she feels she is still penalised in many situations because of the diagnosis of autism. She was convinced that her blind spot moment was during the chickenpox infection, when everything in her life went messed up by her GP.

Simon did not have any hesitation in sharing what he thought was his own blind spot moment, although he warned that between his feelings and the medical reality validated by doctors there was no association at all. He grew up playing football in the field next to the churchyard of his hometown, in Essex. He started at the age of five and went on for years playing football once or twice during the week, and then during the weekends. He could not miss his football training and the matches for anything else. But one day before a decisive match he had an unexplained seizure in front of her parents, after which he did not want to play football anymore. He completely lost interest in the sport. Nobody could explain why, nor discover what happened to him. He was not able to provide any justification. His parents, teachers, classmates, coaches, everybody tried to elicit from him a sign, if not a reason, a clue of whatever kind of accident might have happened to him so that they could make sense of his behaviour. Doctors made thorough investigations as well. Nothing came out. He did not have a memory for the seizure. He remembered, vaguely, that he enjoyed playing football, but did not have anything to say about it, other than apathy: he just did not want to play football anymore. Also watching football or even listen to his friends talking about football would put him in a state his father was afraid could be called, clinically, narcolepsy, because he seemed almost falling asleep, no matter how much excitement was going on around him.

The year after this incident Simon started playing basketball and then he was quite active cycling and swimming, the gym and so on and so forth. Coincidentally or not, in the same period of his seizure he started experiencing gastrointestinal symptoms that were at first dismissed. The following year he was diagnosed as celiac, although years later it turned out he had another autoimmune disease (Crohn's) and non celiac gluten sensitivity. That was Simon's blind spot, and believe it or not, everything started with not playing football anymore for unknown reasons.

He apologised for telling a long story. Everybody, and Brian Gee too, found Simon's blind spot moment, with its mystery attached, absolutely interesting.

Sam said he had a difficult upbringing and several sad memories of his childhood but perhaps his blind spot was when her chemistry teacher in his secondary school called him psychotic, and wrote it down in a report that went to his parents and to other teachers. Since then, the idea that he had a mental illness remained attached to him like a magnet on the fridge, although he believed he never acted in a way less than ordinary. He tended to become upset and irritated at times, or too excited in other occasions, or be the buffoon of certain social situations to keep relatives and friends interested in what he had to say, but to the best of his memory he never lost his temper in any aggressive manner, neither as a young boy nor later on as an adult. However, pretty much in the same period of that sticky judgement it happened that he was diagnosed with Inflammatory Bowel Disease and then with bipolar disorder.

A lady with a bit of a squint and bulging eyes said her blind spot was very likely connected to the relationship with her disabled brother and autistic mother: she grew up convinced she must care for the brother but at a decisive moment other family members took over that role, and at the same time she lost her business and suffered from peptic ulcers and other symptoms during the perimenopause. Then she got a diagnosis of Sjögren's. So perhaps, she said, something went awry in her body at that moment in time when many things abruptly changed at the same time.

The slim lady with parotid enlargement said she wrote down something about her blind spot moment in childhood, after the suicide of her father, but she would rather not to share the particulars of that period in her life. Brian Gee reassured everything was perfectly fine.

The lady next to the slim one had a little pouch on her side, suggesting she was carrying around a stoma. She said without any emotion in her voice that before becoming chronically ill in her adolescence, she had been sexually abused by a professor of her secondary school who had offered her a lift home. Instead, once in the car, he made her performing oral sex on him. She was diagnosed with interstitial lung disease at first and then with several other conditions, including autism.

Faces around the table were speechless after that.

Brian thanked profusely everybody and suggested they continued after a coffee break, in fifteen minutes time.

After the interval several participants declined to share their exercises or said they would do it at a later moment, through the online platform. Three women preferred not to say anything at the moment other than they had been diagnosed with schizophrenia spectrum disorder in their 20s and 30s. Other two middle age ladies diagnosed with Lupus at a young age mentioned sex abuse in connection with mental health problems. A lady with orange dye hair said she had been diagnosed with juvenile arthritis as a teenager but she could not reckon if she has ever had any blind spot at all. Another one had alopecia aereata after a miscarriage, and believed she developed autoimmunity after that. One Scottish lady with vasculitis said she thought her blind spot moment was when she had appendectomy, and curiously enough she mentioned that her sister could have had a similar story to tell because of a diagnosis of Sjögren's and Hashimoto, the symptoms of which, seen in retrospect, started after a tonsillectomy in Tuscany, where they were used to spend the summer holidays.

Simon was completely baffled by the stories looming after that quick round of introductions, showing to him that the horizon of autoimmune diseases was much more varied than he had ever imagined. He felt intrigued to understand more about the lives of his fellow participants: there would be a lot to learn about their journeys through "The Blind Spot" research programme.

Notes

(1) For a comprehensive reference resource about autoimmune diseases see the website of the American Autoimmune Association (autoimmune.org) formerly known as AARDA, an organisation founded in 1991. It publishes a searchable database with links to other

associations of patients or scientific societies for each condition, beside a vast range of documents.

It is generally acknowledged by institutional and clinical authorities that autoimmune diseases, the number of which continues to grow, occur in clusters, very often incurable at present, but treatable through the administration of highly personalised systemic immunomodulator and immunosuppressant drugs. Experimental cell therapies are being developed as well. The majority of patients cope with symptomatic interventions, lifestyle and functional medicine.

For a thorough overview of Sjögren's as it is known and treated by the most accredited clinicians and patients' organisations as of 2022 see: Wallace, D. et al. (editors), *The Sjögren's Book*, Sjögren's Foundation and Oxford University Press, 2022. This books wants to reach the general public but it is not freely accessible over the Internet, nor easily found in public libraries. Conversely, the websites of the USA Sjögren's Foundation and many other national patients associations offer leaflets, booklets, clinical guidelines for free.

For an essay targeted to patients and medics about knowledge management and autoimmune diseases, in particular Sjögren's, see also: Longo, B., The Sicca Messenger, Online Data Assessment, 2025.

(2) The coincidental higher than normal occurrence of autoantibodies in people who present symptoms of schizophrenia spectrum disorder has been fascinating researchers in psychiatry and other disciplines for about a Century. In spite of the high level of skepticism expressed every now and then by authoritative studies that did not find any conclusive evidence for it, the hypothesis that "immune system dysfunction is involved in the pathophysiology of schizophrenia spectrum disorders (SSD)" keeps resurrecting from time to time and anytime that a new biomarker is identified in a cohort of patients with multiple conditions, both autoimmune and psychiatric. See: Gangadin, SS et al, *Immune Dysfunction in Schizophrenia Spectrum Disorders*, Annual Review of Clinical Psychology 2024. 20:229–57; Shiwaku, H, *Autoantibodies and Inflammation in Schizophrenia*, Psychiatry and Clinical Neurosciences, Frontier Review, John Wiley & Sons, 2025; Duan, L. et al, *Causality between autoimmune diseases and schizophrenia: a bidirectional Mendelian randomization study*, BMC Psychiatry (2024) 24:817.

The Sun's Kisses

I arrive five minutes earlier but there isn't any space left in the bicycles rack next to the entrance. So I go back to the high street to find a lamp post. I enter the auditorium while somebody is still instructing the public through health and safety.   Students still greeting each other. I am not the only mature attendee though: some ladies of my age perch down from the back of the theatre. A power point slide with the title of the lecture appears on the big screen while I take a seat at the end of a back row, where I can stretch my knees.

Various pictures flicker in a rapid succession. I need to adjust my glasses. Today I find too much light is annoying me, in spite of the turned-down brim of my hat.

The professor is young, tall, smiling persistently. A handsome guy. He kicks off quizzing the audience about a giant claw flashing on the screen. Some students reply enthusiastically in a ping pong of names of animals. Nope nope nope. We are all hooked by what seems an exhibit for a photographic prize.   Interesting, from many points of view, but not my thing. I came here to learn, and to be entertained is part of it, although my thirst for knowledge has become impatience: my tolerance for whatever does not give me answers straightaway is quite low.

There is something about keratins that truly and deeply upsets me, like I have to confront a truth denied to me for the whole of my life: I am sixty years old now and suspects keratins play a role also in my kidney issues.

I know there are chances that attending public lectures will not give me any definitive answer, because academics cannot really say if autoimmunity is caused by genetic defects that mess up keratinisation processes in the body, for instance, or anything else one is exposed too in life, starting from heavy lights. But I hope what I have learned will become clearer: browsing tons of clinical literature with the tools of my own lived experience is at times very confusing, and tiring.

I want to know more about my sun's pebbles: that is why I am here. My dad called them this way. The scientific name, perhaps less romantic, is milia. Dermatologists define them as small, whitish cysts made of keratin. (1)

In various English dictionaries milia are presented as "blocked sebaceous glands", clearly something dysfunctional as the word "blocked" suggests. Other popular web pages talk about "milk spots", making less clear they can become inflamed, and infected too, and are not so innocent.

All in all, dictionaries and reference books do not provide any answer to the question I asked my father almost sixty years ago: why do these white hard spots appear just under or on top of the skin? And where do they come from?

My sun's pebbles were a constant of the summer on legs and arms. Dad explained they were nothing to be worried about, just a sign I had been kissed by the sun. It was a lyrical image that mesmerised me for years.

Growing up, I did not bother to ask for a more plausible rationale: the cysts were minuscules and harmless. The idea of being kissed by the sun was lovely enough.

Some pebbles would quickly disappear during the following autumn and winter, so that I would completely forget them before the next summer. Other little cysts would set in for months, or even years, before I could notice they had gone away silently as they came. After the menarche, the seasonal coming and going of sun's pebbles stopped. We spent less time by the sea during the summer, as my parents divorced and we went to live in separate towns with mum.

After the menopause, they seem to have come back in less innocuous, much subtle, almost invisible, forms, in strange places, like through the excruciating inflammation of the cornea of the eyes - a condition called keratitis - or the cast in the urine, and those bigger versions of subcutaneous hard spots on the sole of the feet, plus various other annoying minimal acne here and there. Keratinocytes - cells made of this protein - account for up 95% of the cells of the epidermis so that is does not surprise me that something persistently wrong in these cells creates chronic systemic disease.

The professor projects the photo of a mummy from a famous museum asking the audience to guess if the skull is covered by a bespoke wig made to attract visitors or by the mummy's original hair.   The audience laughs. He laughs too. I must be the only one that does not see any fun at all. He then explains the chemical reasons for the longevity of the mummy's hair, with some big "K" recurring in the draws he shows on the screen, illustrating the Keratin distribution in epithelia of various human tissue. In the late 19th Century scientists with diverse backgrounds discovered that different body parts in mammals - hair, feathers, hooves, whalebone - were all made of the same substance. It was then that the study of 'horn' or 'keratin' started, in modern sense. However, it took another century to discover that keratins actually take different forms, called for instance granules and filaments. Keratins coexist forming different architectures in different mammals, and body parts of the same species: the substance is organised in layers connected together through different shapes and structures.

The formula of the amino acid cysteine punch me in the stomach. It seems an unnecessary, distracting technicality but I guess it is relevant for the students.

I wonder if I had enough breakfast.

A snapshot from another age hijacks my mind: I hear myself asking "Dad when do we stop for the ricotta?" in his Ford car. It must have been 1968 or even later, 1970.

We were going to the beach with the lido. The beach was beautiful but our treat was the playground at the lido with the swimming pool: a symbol of luxury, we could afford to go there. We were experiencing the Italian economic boom, with all the amenities and industrial developments much more associated with the north of the country.

Halfway through the journey, papà would stop the car at a small cheese farm, among olive and orange trees: he would buy each of us a little ricotta. Swallowing the wobbly cheese, still warm, from the little basket cases, was an unforgettable thrill. There was no clue I could have a genetic lactose intolerance at the time, although it was clear I needed sheep and goats milk: for several years growing up I avoided cow milk, at least until that precious grandmotherly advice went lost in family quarrels.

The little ricotta was one of the delicious things we would indulge with going to the seaside with dad. Another one was to stop the car along the road and harvest wild prickly pears: these would sometimes require mum's surgery with tweezers in the evening, to remove bristles from our fingers. But it was great fun.

The next slide brings me back to today.

The professor is explaining the loss of function in genetic diseases that involve keratins. Mutations of keratin genes, he is saying, can cause conditions like corneal dystrophy or epidermolysis bullosa (5). Oh dear, it sounds horrible stuff compared to my occasional carbuncles: I am glad that mine are minor and unusual, yet mysterious, skin peculiarities compared to these painful abnormalities. With a rapid slideshow he wants to recap something, possibly to remind students specific points in his syllabus: it starts quoting inflammatory acne, that in turns triggers bacterial overgrowth. Good he does it! I think people, including medics and academics, do not often see that the very cause of a hidden pain can be an inflamed microscopic pustule on the inner layer of the epithelia, inside the body, something that may remain silent and undetectable for months or years, for instance within the minimal renal tubules or in the incredibly rich, and invisible, nerves inside the eyes and their orbits.

There are innumerable other diseases much less known in dermatology that depend on keratinisation, the professor hints commenting another rapid succession of pictures: from xerosis to lichenification, passing through various forms of ichthyosis, they are all not much researched so far, in case somebody is pondering a PhD project on the subject (talk with him later during the reception).

The pictures do not even look as human skin to me: they could be photos of reptiles or geological fossils. I keep on being distracted and tapping on my smartphone, voraciously trying to catch up with the meaning of words I am not familiar with, although I already know that milia have been studied as manifestations of sarcoidosis, Sjögren's, bullous pemphigoid, infantile hemangiomas and so on and so forth - all weird diseases, mostly autoimmune.

The professor enters into more complicated elucidations of some chemicals. And I am lost.

I feel I have almost reached the point of saturation of my attention span when I hear him saying that a recent case report has revealed keratins can have a protective role against cancer. The news of a breakthrough tugs my attention back in: while studying the formation of skin tumours, the professor explains, scientists have "hypothesised that milia originate from the hair bulge of the outer root sheath" (2).

I am lost again with the references to a number of "K" alleles he cites very quickly. This public lecture is a roller coaster. I swallow some irritation, and I quickly google again some of these other "K" while he speaks.

I think it would be fairer towards all members of the public that attend these open lectures if speakers avoided jargon. Anyhow, I am not here to question educational formats, nor academic policies. At its core, science communication is conciseness that leads to an empowered, better quality of life, but I have to concede that human vocabulary is the Achille's heel of the whole endeavour. Either you own it or you do not. I studied some notions of biology in my secondary school 45 years ago: it was another world.

I get that all those "K" numbers refer to different molecules: that's why the word should actually be used in the plural form, because it comprises mixtures of various substances an not only proteins - the keratins, precisely - like the bits and pieces called 'keratin filament-associated proteins (KPAS)' and enzymes. This is why scientists use to talk about K1, K7, K8, K10, K14, K15, K16, K17, K18, K19 etc. (3)

So, I wonder which gene was possibly linked to my sun's pebbles? I know, I know this question is really useless (4): in good or in bad health everything in life is polygenic. However, the temptation of asking the question is irresistible: not a second later, a young woman vigorously raises and waves her hand to get attention. The professor answers pointing to more chemistry. It sounds just cruel to me. Flashing lights from the screen hit my glasses.

He is showing again, rapidly, a sequence of pictures of objects and body parts: keratins are both the solid and sturdy proteins in the sheath that covers horns AND the bendable and soft leather for bags shoes and belts made from the skin of reptiles. It's like he is saying: you stupid, you do not understand the basics here. The variety explains why when you google the subject you find tons of non pertinent web pages publicising toiletries and cosmetics. This substance is everywhere. The hair of mammals, weaved or knitted to make garments, is made of keratins like human hair.

"All good until something gets extremely ... corny - excuse the pun", the professor concludes and he keeps laughing to his own jokes. I think everybody has now got it and he should move on. Keratins are responsible for dysfunctional processes in the body called keratinisation or cornification of the skin. Corneous tissues create problems for human health but they remain quite a niche of limited interest in biological sciences, so far.

I agree: not even GPs understand what I talk about when I try to explain the skin tickening around the nails, and becoming excessively thinner in other parts of the body, exposed to cracks and bruises of all sorts. Minimal scratches here and there that do not heal easily, or bleed abnormally, or appear with black and blue marks without reasons are very frequent in older people and do not get investigated until it may be too late. Other skin abnormalities can develop from deposit of amyloid that could be mistaken for milia, the professor explains.

Some of his points are easy to understand, for instance that keratinocytes are always on the move: they travel from the inner layers towards the surface of the body, after which they will be finally discarded. Other considerations, I would argue, sound a waste of energy, meaningless even if you are an expert, and may require to restructure the definition of the problem (if any). My GP, for instance, years ago, was unable to explain what could be a cellulite nodule, a swollen lymph node or a keratoacanthoma, that is a nodule made with a jam of keratin cells, perhaps crushed on their journey towards the surface of the skin. To me, that was just a big, hard and infected, stubborn carbuncle that needed antibiotics. Unless the bulge is bigger than a certain number of millimetres, the GP said, there is no reason to treat it or investigate it further. Wait and see was his recommended line of …inaction. I insisted to take antibiotics and eventually the bulge went away, after several weeks. Unbelievable you need to treat a carbuncle with oral antibiotics, isn't it? In another occasion I had one of these big pustules on the groin, so painful I could hardly walk and eventually it required incision and drainage, not just antibiotics, thanks to emergency surgery.

Something really interesting in respect of autoimmunity wake up my attention: degenerated keratin cells can form what the professor calls amyloid deposits under the skin. These can become even worse if you start rubbing them, because auto-antibodies come along on the site of the bulge, and release more fighting cells: oh dear. in the effort, they release an enzyme the by-product of which - surprise surprise - consists of amyloid K.

Wow. I remain simply fascinated by the whole description, having the hunch that an instance of such aberrant phenomenon is what is happening in my body, from time to time.

Then the professor enters another world of chemistry, again, to explain that primary localised cutaneous amyloidosis is a disease of the skin - probably what I fear. - in which because of scratching (or other subtle, and complex reason) a bulge becomes a type of ulcerated nodule, itching, painful, sometimes bleeding, sometimes getting infected and releasing pus, requiring antibiotics and a long time to heal (4). That's it. I know it.

The following slide gives me some further satisfaction because I got it right: dysfunctional keratinisation processes are common to several granulomatous diseases, including autoimmune conditions like sarcoidosis, or infectious diseases like lupus vulgaris or leishmaniasis (5).

Images of amyloid deposits under the microscope should reveal the cells structure and chain: amyloid deposits in the internal organs can lead to progressive loss of function and even cause death whereas on the surface of the skin most of the times the problem is seen as an aesthetic nuisance: brittle nails, heavy eyelids, ticker and harder skin on the fingers, blistering here and there. Oh, do not tell me anything about the fingers. Perhaps this explains why since I was a child I have been so prone to cuticles overgrowth, with lot of dry and peeling skin around the nails. I had the awful habit of biting and chewing the excess, peeling skin - in the attempt to halt the problem. During some stressful times, the compulsive habit really reached the embarrassing point of giving me bleeding fingers or fingers covered in plasters for days.

Nobody ever offered me any treatment for this skin problem, because it was framed as a psychological compulsive disorder called dermatophagia. However, at a certain point in my busy young adult life, around the age of 25, I realised that biting my overgrown skin was an issue not at all caused only by anxiety. The peeling skin, the dry and falling apart cuticles were exposing me to increasing risks of bacterial or fungal infections. So slowly slowly I trained myself to avoid biting them.

Overgrown and cracked bits and pieces of skin have appeared also around the toenails and even on the sole of the feet after the menopause. Could the very root of the problem be in all those sun's kisses I received when I was a toddler, spending too much time by the sea?

This part of the lecture enters technicalities that are quite tough to grab: these skin abnormalities are due to cytokines (stuff called IL-6 and IL-10), released at a fast pace as an inflammatory response. That means, I understand, that on one side they trigger autoimmunity (more B and T cells coming to useless battles, fought on the skin, overreacting to nothing); but on the other side they attract more actual, real enemies, such as fungi, viruses or bacteria.

The professor has interrupted its fast sequence of very technical, boring slides to answer another urgent question from a student. I did not catch it, but in response he shows photos from another power point file on his laptop. This time around he chooses visuals of scientists, pioneers that in the 1970s and 1980s investigated keratins, mentioning nuclear magnetic resonance - a technology that became common to see and study the structure of keratins only around the mid 2000s. I get the gist: modern study of keratins started with Francis Crick research on sheep hair, the wool.

I smile to myself: the ricotta cheese gets in the way of my attention span, once again.

One minuscule pietra di sole I was tormenting, scratching, and even try to squeeze at all times without success when I was little was in the front middle of my left thigh. It lasted for years. I eventually won that battle: at some point it came out without too much squeezing, it just surrendered to my will. However, an immutable open pore remained in the skin in its place, to remind me every time I look at it how stupid we can be fighting something we do not understand: it is like a miniature well in my thigh, the sign that a kiss of the sun might have landed as a nano-meteorite, invaded the hair follicle, then vanished in a microscopic abyss, where all the proteins must come from.

Three or more sun pebbles appeared after the menarche on my breasts. That was scary. They grew during the following years, minimally, but it was enough to cause me great worrying for some time: I feared my breasts could turn into monstrous boobs, not only bigger compared to many classmates but also with multiple nipples developing from the sun kisses I had not asked for. (6)

Even today I get that slightly frightening sensation when I see minimal cysts on the eyelids appearing and luckily enough disappearing often in a matter of days, if not hours. Sometimes a swim, a sauna, a shower or just washing my face with sterile salted water eliminates them in seconds. But they can persist creating more dryness and grittiness, and more anxiety, and more opportunities for infections. My vision gets blurred, and tired. Such milia appear, coincidentally, here and there in the body at a time in which also other major symptoms appear - like gastrointestinal dysfunctions. Cysts on the eyelids, erythema on the torso, boils on legs, urinary cast... what a hell of a trait d'union is behind among all these "minimal" epithelia peculiarities, we are not allowed to call "abnormalities" according to the rheumatologist? why such "peculiar" keratinisation process does not attract any medical interest, being considered nothing really serious?

The sun pebbles appearing on my eyelids are like minuscule bombardiers coming from an inner fortress in my bloodstream. They must tell something. They seem messengers who dare coming through, announcing that a flare-up is either coming or ongoing, or just brushing away with almost no disturb, like they were used to do long ago, during the summer months of my childhood.

A pebble appeared at some point in my early teens and that has remained steadily, firmly triumphant in its place since then, but for becoming slightly bigger after the menopause. It is still annoying today as it was when I was playing the 45-rpm single vinyl record by The Hues Corporation "Rock the boat", dancing in front of the mirror in my grandmother's room. If I look at it now, at home or in the mirror of a lift for instance, while I am trimming my hair or just going around for shopping in a department store full of mirrors, my concentration risks to get stuck on it, and I cannot continue to do whatever for long seconds or minutes, asking myself what the hell is causing this pebble on my skin? For many years I wanted, I tried to get rid of it, squeezing it, scratching it. No way. Imperturbable, immovable. But now it is just a part of me, it is totally at ease with my body, solidly implanted in the soft wrinkled layer of skin in the front middle of my neck, at the bottom of the thyroid cartilages. Indeed, it could have suggested to check my thyroid antibodies early on. More than a sun kiss it reminds me the image of a tear dropped from the thyroid gland that remained stuck inside the skin, a spark from the larynx preparing to scream at some point. A petrified kiss of the sun, or my father's kiss. Will that tear, dropped ages ago, become another autoimmune disease in my later life? When I touch it and I close my eyes, I can still see the beach in the background, and me and my brother playing with dad in the swimming pool of the lido.

Over the reception (white or red wine, lot of orange juice and soda water, peanuts and crisps - nothing I can eat or drink but tap water from a broach nicely put in the corner of a table) I am approached by an elderly couple. They were seated in the row in front of me in the lecture theatre. Friendly over 60 I would say. We have a cordial chat but I cannot stay.

I try to be as much extrovert and talkative as I remember I was until just few years ago, but I would really like to go out in the sunshine, have a rice cake or a banana: the air conditioning is killing me, and my fingertips have been freezing for a while now, urging me action.

I make my way to the exit. The warm air caresses my face and arms, dried out inside the auditorium.

I often cut my ride short, taking the bicycle on the train. But I prefer to ride back home tonight. The warm breeze at sunset calms the skin after the exposure to the cold air conditioning. The blood pressure must be returning to a more comfortable level.

Passed the Imperial War Museum I stop to get rid of my jumper, as the body temperature seems now restored, the heat returned to my fingers and forearms, skull, feet.

The image of the beach comes back. Was nice to feel the sun on the skin, wasn't it? I ask to myself. Those were long days, perhaps just too long, perhaps too much iodine. We laid down in the sunshine, playing with sand castles for hours.

There was no idea that something could ever be wrong.

My father did not know anything about keratins. He chose the best words for my imagination: my sun pebbles were minuscule, but fascinating milia that could not be squeezed, picked, scratched in any way. They seemed made of stone fragments fallen from the stars, harder than any earthy or sea dust, landed on my skin, kissed by the sun.

Notes

(1) Clinical literature and various websites offer definitions and images of milia, categorised as milia en plaque, milia post-photodermatitis, multiple eruptive milia and milia post-trauma, some

of which may be removed nowadays with CO2 laser vaporisation. Descriptions and photos for "miliaria crystallina" or "clear heat rash" are abundant, reassuring about their benign and almost unnoticeable nature. It is only within more advanced studies of genomics and molecular biology that we can find evidence of the role of keratins in pre- and postnatal development of epithelial tissues. A synthetic definition reflecting the state of knowledge is offered by the American National Institute of Health within the StatPearls encyclopaedia: "Milia (singular: milium) - they write - are benign and transient dermal cysts of keratin that present as small firm white papules in various numbers most commonly distributed on the face, but they can also be present on other anatomical areas such as the upper trunk, extremities, and genital area (prepuce). The classification of milia includes primary and secondary. The vast majority of primary milia accounts for congenital milia that occur spontaneously and are present at birth, mainly over the nose, scalp, eyelids, cheeks, gum border (Bohn nodules), and palate (Epstein pearls). Still, there is another percentage of primary milia that may occur in association with certain rare genodermatoses (inherited genetic skin disorders) in children and adults. Meanwhile, secondary milia manifest in association with underlying skin pathology, medications, or skin trauma". See: Gallardo Avila PP, Mendez MD. *Milia*. 2022 Aug 8. In: StatPearls (Internet). StatPearls Publishing; 2022 Jan–. Interesting complementary descriptions of how keratinisation process occur in the human body can be found in: Moll, R et al, *The human keratins: biology and pathology*, in Histochem Cell Biol, 2008, 6:705-733; Shaheen, B et al, *Corneal Nerves in Health and Disease*, Surv Ophthalmol, (59) 2014, 3: 263–285

(2) Kurokawa, I et al, *Milia may originate from the outermost layers of the hair bulge of the outer root sheath: A case report*, Oncology Letters, 12: 5190-5192, 2016.

(3) The authors of a 2012 review on keratinisation write: "In humans, there are around 30 keratin families divided into two groups, namely, acidic and basic keratins, which are arranged in pairs. - the authors explain. - They are expressed in a highly specific pattern related to the epithelial type and stage of cellular differentiation. A total of 54 functional genes exist which codes for these keratin families. The expression of specific keratin genes is regulated by the differentiation of epithelial cells within the stratifying squamous epithelium.

Mutations in most of these genes are now associated with specific tissue fragility disorders which may manifest both in skin and mucosa depending on the expression pattern. The keratins and keratin-associated proteins are useful as differentiation markers because their expression is both region specific and differentiation specific. Antibodies to keratin are considered as important tissue differentiation markers and therefore are an integral aid in diagnostic pathology." See Shetty, S and Gokul S., *Keratinisation and its Disorders*, Oman Medical Journal (2012) Vol. 27, No. 5: 348-357.

(4) Clinical literature, particularly from dermatology, has extensively reported cases of primary localised cutaneous nodular amyloidosis (PLCNA) among patients of connective tissue diseases, particularly in Sjögren's disease. In this condition, frequent generic skin issues are seen more frequently than in the healthy population, from eczema to purpura on limbs, from urticarial vasculitis to non-Hodgkin's lymphoma. It has been proposed that physicians should rule out associated Sjögren's disease in patients with PLCNA and vice-versa. See: Llamas-Molina, J.M. et al, *Localized Cutaneous Nodular Amyloidosis: A Specific Cutaneous Manifestation of Sjögren's Syndrome*, Int. J. Mol. Sci. 2023, 24, 7378; Wang, Y et el, *Primary Localized Cutaneous Nodular Amyloidosis Presenting as Milia: An Unusual Clinical Manifestation*, Clin. Cosmet. Investig. Dermatol. 2022, 15, 1639–1642.

(5) For an updated catalogue of associations between genetic defects and keratinisation abnormalities see: Poli, MC et al, *Human inborn errors of immunity: 2024 update on the classification from the International Union of Immunological Societies Expert Committee*, J. Hum. Immun. 2025 Vol. 1 No. 1. See also: Bardhan, A et al., *Epidermolysis bullosa*, Nat Rev Dis Primers 6, 78 (2020)

(6) Milia around the nipples are more or less normal areolar glands also called Montgomery tubercles after the obstetrician who first described them in 1837. A Wikipedia page explains that these tubercles "make oily secretions (lipoid fluid) that keep the areola and the nipple lubricated and protected".

The Lazy Eye

I met Evan on a walk long ago. We exchanged phone numbers. Then we lost contact for few years, after I moved south of the river. I had a knee ligaments injury, and for some time I could not walk but for physiotherapy and strolls. It takes time to recover.

I would not say we have a romantic, nor a sexual relationship. It is something that soothes the soul. Perhaps I should use the word friendship.

Evan is a kind man. His wrinkled face and the severity of his jaw are not very attractive, but he has his own way to conquer sympathy and admiration. He has an encyclopaedic memory. He worked as historian and curator in a science and technology museum for over thirty years until he was sacked: the management wanted fresh blood for their public engagement programme so they promoted a young blogger (content creator, they say) to his post, and offered him to be re-hired and retrained in building security, that made no sense to him. He opted for an early retirement option, a less stressful change, although not very convenient financially. Then he started doing freelance casual jobs in the community. He is now a very requested handyman in north London: plumbing, carpentry, gardening, moving furniture, that type of things.

We share a sort of cultural sensitiveness, and vast curiosity for anything science. He is a vegan too, so I do not have to worry about barbecues if I ask him to go out.

Sometimes we have conversations that could deserve a podcast, we joke, if only anybody paid us as content creators or science communicators.

We laugh a lot about our common today's nothingness in the world of knowledge transfer, a field in which we were well respected professionals, back in the day.

The nervousness outweighs the pleasure to see Evan tonight, because of an appalling last minute change of programme. My fault, and it is quite frustrating. We had tickets for a ballet at the theatre, that we both like very much. Then, last night, I've got a phone call from my neighbour Wendy, a retired nurse with plenty of energy and community spirit, as they call it.

Wendy and I volunteer for an educational programme within our local National Health Service trust. In fairness, I do very little. I miss out nine out of ten meetings. I just said, few years ago, at the time of my autoimmune diagnosis, that I was keen to help, offering research, medical news - that sort of things. I worked as a librarian for almost thirty years: pin down and sharing reliable information comes easy.

Wendy keeps me posted: monthly meetings, everything interesting happening in the neighbourhood, updates about all the talks she organises, with guests speakers coming in person or via video-links, and so on and so forth. The themes of the meetings are often problems I have mentioned to her *en passant*, when I met her around at shops or at the local train station.

She called yesterday to remind she is going to chair an event at our local surgery tonight. The theme is "The lazy eye", something I suggested to her last year. You did not forget it, did you? I could not say that yes, I did.

Bloody hell. I could not say I wanted to go to the ballet instead.

Evan did not show a second of resentment: "No problem at all, let's go for it, it may be fun".

Evan is really easy to be friend with. He knows about my obsession with the aetiology of autoimmune diseases, connecting the dots about symptoms, in particular those impacting eyes and vision.

We meet at my local pub, next to the station for a shandy (him) and a green tea (me).

Evan has an interest in all sorts of medical issues from the perspective of history of science, that I also find a fascinating window on professionalism and human nature. He is genuinely keen on going and listening to the talk.

We have both laughed several times at scientific papers about specific medical problems that I have researched, including amblyopia. We know how things are made up, to satisfy expectations in terms of evidence, or returns on investments in research, all important notions entrenched in academic as well as in public policy practices, that are not exempt from bias, design errors, vested interests. Since the age of enlightenment, when statistics came along, some scientists would rather cut their fingers than concede their measurements can be wrong.

Some doctors are becoming more relaxed and appreciative of the contributions citizen scientists can bring, especially in fields like cancer and rare diseases, but overall, as patients, we are all utterly patronised and not listened to even in a participatory or community context. Fact is that the scientific method has been struggling for centuries to demonstrate whatsoever in respect of some conditions, it just goes on with empirical remedies, like occlusion for the lazy eye.

When I first talked to Evan about amblyopia - that is the medical term for the lazy eye - he told me there was a time, until more or less a century ago, in which medics thought amblyopia was essentially an intoxication: one could catch it simply eating potatoes or drinking alcohol, or ingesting the wrong drugs. Then became also evident it could be a iatrogenic disease.

Evan sent me the digital editions of books by professors of ophthalmology, written in the late 1800s, with detailed accounts of what we would call today ocular injures caused by poisons and toxic substances. These must have been frequent at the time of fast industrial progress, with no healthy and safety at all. The unfortunate patients could end up blind while they were hoping to heal an injury or a partial sight loss. For few decades those cases remained known as cases of "toxic or alcoholic amblyopia", often hiding the fact that might have been caused by doctors trying to cure the abnormal binocular vision, or a squint (1).

Less entertaining perhaps, but not less curious, is the fact that still today the preferred cure for amblyopia consists in suppressing the vision of the good eye with patches, a method that more or less in its current form was devised in the 18th Century. The controversial theory behind it says that a forced occlusion of the good eye allows the brain to learn how to use the input from the lazy eye. In more recent years, clinical trials and large studies showed that this old-fashioned, empirical method, has actually its partial scientific validity. Reasons for its efficacy and failures have become clearer. The failures arise from the fact that often the lazy eye has been affected since the early months of life by something or the lack of something - permanently.

Evan is about to say something he has recently discovered about amblyopia when my phone buzzes: it is a text from Wendy, saying the room is getting full, where are you? I text back: "On my way".

We do not know exactly who is coming to Wendy's "community seminar", as she called it. We joke at the idea of pub goers or heavy drinkers suddenly becoming all interested in history of ophthalmology. And off we go.

"Perhaps you should say this is your meeting, Clara, managed by Wendy", Evan smiles while we leave the pub. We are going to walk through the park.

"Well, yes, but I do feel slightly guilty, because, you know, I actually do not volunteer at all as I promised. I just drop ideas from time to time, and she takes from there".

Evan entertains me again on the history of the term, the etymology of which means, literary, dull eye: "Did you tell Wendy that the first to use the term amblyopia, or amaurosis, was Hippocrates, the father of medicine?"

"Ah, no... well it doesn't surprise me, but no, I did not know it. What is amaurosis by the way? A synonym?", I am genuinely surprised I haven't heard of it, or I do not remember it.

"Ancient Greek word for obscuring, perhaps alluding to the cure more than to the problem? Amazing that in the fourth Century BC, Hippocrates already referred to this condition in which they knew there was no actual disease of the eye but only evidence of a diminished visual acuity, or loss of sight. Then another greek medic, Galen, two centuries later, and almost one millennium later an Arab doctor, Haly Abbas, came to the same conclusion".

"Oh dear, it is you that Wendy should have asked to come and give us a lecture about the history of the lazy eye." I hint, quite seriously. We often tease each other this way.

Evan never lose his coolness: "Do you think the experts she found will talk about the history of amblyopia?", is his nonchalance reaction.

"I do not know, but I do not think so. She agreed some prerecorded videos, so we cannot even ask questions to the speakers, because they had other commitments somewhere else and could not make it in person….. Oh, Evan - I cannot contain my frustration - I am so sorry we do not go to the ballet. You know, this is unlikely the sort of event I had imagined… I would have liked somebody talking about new developments of the immune cells found in the eyes, discussing my idea of a possible connection between the lazy eye and autoimmune diseases like Sjögren's or Myasthenia or Thyroid Eye Disease…"

"And…?"

"Well, apparently Wendy was told that this was a very arguable approach to a theme for a patients engagement event… we cannot have a community event around complex issues". I am feeling battered by the evident impossibility of genuine, quality driven, useful science communication. I see the community engagement programme as a total waste of public funding, in truth.

"Ah, money money money" Evan smiles. He understood I am a bit nervous, so he tries to flex our conversation towards a more lighthearted chat. I am not in that mood though.

"We cannot even have live experts - I continue - the truth is they cost too much and we are just a small local group", I add. My disappointment has perhaps reached a point of no return and I haven't realised before tonight.

"Well, it is true that amblyopia today tends to be researched as a neurodevelopment disorder, in demand of billion of investments for new studies into such an old issue…But I guess there would not be many doctors willing to come to a local community meeting and talk to patients about these new R&D approaches… I am with you anyhow… she could have asked a PhD student, or a young doctor… there isn't scientific complexity that cannot be explained in plain terms, is it?"

Evan often finishes my thoughts, or paraphrases words I have left hanging in the air.

"Yes", I conclude. I know I'd better calm down my frustration: "I read scientists believe the lazy eye develops very early in life, before the age of 6 or 7, often because of an undetected and uncorrected astigmatism at birth, or an injury soon after. But if something prevents a child's eye to fully develop, I wonder if there is any chance that also the immune system gets involved and trapped in some way…"

Evan continues my hypothetical reasoning: "Or it could be that an unknown genetic condition causes the lazy eye in the first place… It may stay otherwise silent for years, and perhaps it manifests in old age through systemic, autoimmune dysfunctions…is this what you are thinking?"

"Yes, I was thinking something like that. It would have been fascinating to learn about these associations. So far the only genetic condition amblyopia has been associated with, as far as I have understood, is Turner syndrome, that causes severe developmental problems in children, not only sight impairment. But there are so many other genetic conditions with underlying vision problems, and other developments in molecular medicine, you know…" (2).

We are almost there but Evan does not want to give up on our common curiosity so he slows down to ask me, a bit flattering: "Clara, the idea that a lazy eye can be the sign of an autoimmunity process settling into the eyes is fascinating. It should be investigated further … we should talk about this with some scientists, I mean real experts we can meet in person."

"Well", I look into Evan's eyes. "I do not know… there must be or there could be something important there… it is exactly what I tried to explain to Wendy last year.   I did not find any definitive, clear answer to these questions but I have had a hunch that there may be something non totally convincing in the way the entire issue of amblyopia has been framed so far…. A genetic cause for amblyopia has been completely excluded so far, but… you know… It is like the story of the immune privilege of the eye. Scientists were convinced there is no immune system in the eye and then that turned out totally bonkers." (3).

"Absurd not to talk about it" Evans concludes. My thought exactly.

"Indeed", I say "but you know… Wendy said she was told these are subjects too complex for our local events… Anyhow… Let's go" I say, accelerating the pace. It is really getting late.

Wendy comes to hug me while I am still in the hall: "Clara. Darling. Nice to see you".

I smile introducing Evan.

"What a great surprise you brought someone else with you too, well done.".

Wendy arranged the chairs in a semicircle, and there are not less than twenty five people, that is a big number: other meetings have registered 6 to 15 people on average.

I have a look around. I reckon some visually impaired neighbours. A person I always meet at the supermarket came with his usual buddy. I recognise some other familiar faces.

We sit in the front row, opposite to the small podium were Wendy is ready to start. She is about to speak, but the mic does not work. I am not sure she really needs a microphone. She absolutely wants it so she goes in search of somebody acting technician for the evening, that could be able to fix it.

I look at Evan and he smiles at me, perhaps we are thinking the same about Wendy's outfit and perfume. She is overdressed, in red, with a dress that would be alright for an evening at the theatre in the West End. She put on too much geranium essence too.

She doesn't look at all 72, but for the reddish hair dye, that I find slightly ridiculous, and the heavy breathing of a person of her age who is overweight. If I did not know her, I would never say she is credible at all in this role.

I whisper into Evan's ear: "I am sorry, we could have gone to the ballet."

"She looked so happy to see you here", he whispers back.

"How did you discover you had a lazy eye?" Wendy asked me last year. Very simply. Somehow, it must have been a day of great calm in the family, I noticed I could not read with my left eye. I read a lot as a child. Reading would give me comfort, company and calm feelings, while I looked after my disabled brother who would imitate me at all times. While our parents were deeply entrapped in their constant fight against each other, against relatives, and against the world, before their legal separation, we would retreat in our room and just read books. I was about 9 years old and I still remember I was reading a very impressive book for children I had borrowed at school, *Il gran sole di Hiroshima*, about the atomic bomb. That night I said to my parents, at the dinner table, that I was unable to read with the left eye. Very agitated, my mother somehow in despair, they brought me immediately to be seen by an ophthalmologist the day after. We had to travel for few hours as in those days ophthalmology clinics were still a rarity in the South of Italy. And then I went through the typical routine prescribed to children in these cases, patching the good eye. Glasses and occlusion. I kept on doing it for one entire year, without any improvement.

The astigmatism, and the partial loss sight from the lazy eye, had already settled in, and remained stubbornly always the same since then, for the whole of my life so far: blurred and slightly distorted, the vision from the left eye never worsened or improved since then. But I always had great care from ophthalmologists and opticians, especially after we moved to the North of Italy. I did not develop any sign of strabismus for at least another decade, or I'd better say that I probably had what specialists tend to call heterophoria, a latent strabismus, a sort of menace of squint. (4)

It was only in my 20s that I started to notice a slightly outward intermittent squint appearing and disappearing more often, ramping up if I was particularly tired, but not changing anything in terms of visual acuity. All the opticians that visited me over five decades could not explain why I did not have a permanent squint, or a permanent double vision.

"So it took a while before you noticed something that actually started much earlier", Wendy asked me several times. She seemed puzzled by the idea that strabismus and sight problems may not occur together and that parents may not be aware that a toddler has a poor sight.

"But today you have a squint coming and going" she remarked, confused by the fact that lazy eye, squint, double vision, and other visual acuity issues may all have different aetiologies, and not necessarily occur together. Wendy was hoping I would talk about the complaint I had made after a disappointing experience at the hospital, because of a possible allergic reaction to the drops they put in my eyes for a fundoscopy. It would have been a waste of time, protracting sufferance, humiliation and accusations of being paranoid, since I had no evidence they had made anything wrong. The only thing I could complain about, as I did, was the prescription of an antibiotic that is known to cause adverse reactions in Lupus.

Never mind, here we are. It seems the microphone does not work, not even after the acting technician intervention.

"I think we can hear you and the videos too", I say to her, revealing a sort of impatience.

Eventually Wendy is convinced she can start, forgetting the faulty mic.

She kicks off the meeting very professionally, talking about the "community spirit" at the heart of this programme, then reading a definition of astigmatism that is projected on the screen behind her. She says that this is what we can find in any eye's physiology textbook, describing astigmatism as a refractive error, relatively common across various ethnic groups, "in which the focal length of the lens or the cornea is different in different planes. This causes a point image to become a line, and blurs the image as a whole. The easiest way to cure this is to use astigmatic glasses in which the powers in different planes are complementary to those of the eye itself". (5)

Wendy presses the button on the remote and the documentary begins with a close-up: the ophthalmologist interviewed is a Dr Philip Young PhD. While he speaks, captions appear superimposed in bold lettering with definitions and references.

The best way to understand astigmatism - Dr Young explains - is to refer to "imperfections in the curve of the corneal surface which make the bending of light (refraction) uneven in different parts of the cornea: you can be born with some astigmatism or you can develop it because of corneal problems such as injury or scarring. Surgery of the eye, for example corneal grafting, cataract and glaucoma operations, can produce unwanted astigmatism. Another cause of astigmatism is if the lens within the eye, the natural one or the plastic form introduced at cataract surgery, is not quite in the ideal position. Appropriate correction for astigmatism is incorporated into your glasses or contact lenses by the optometrist" (5). Etcetera, etcetera.

After a while the interviewer asks Dr Young what are the "appropriate corrections" at what age. The way in which the brain adapts to astigmatism is incredibly interesting, Dr Young continues. Recent studies have even questioned we really understand the neurological and retinal implications of amblyopia, besides its association with the astigmatic eye (6).

I find his way of talking evasive, even confusing, for instance when he adds that "amblyopia is a non-genetic condition, but amblyogenic factors may have a genetic basis" (7). What we know for certain is that as an early response to strabismus the brain turns off input form that lazy eye, he says. That's pretty much all: experts talk about suppression of the information coming from the lazy eye, that is very often distorted and disturbing, so that the visual cortex gets no noise. The video continues with Dr Young citing other case histories that do not say anything really new, at least to me: according to medical knowledge, what happened in my childhood was that my brain shut down the eye in order not to compromise the vision with double shapes or other distortions etcetera. I am not convinced.

Someone else is not convinced either: a 40-sh years old lady intervenes saying that families experience an awful lack of standardisation of treatment for children with squint. Current medical advice, she says, seems a patchy collection of guidelines developed on empirical basis, pointing to occlusion, spectacles or a choice of activities and exercises, with specialists often contradicting each other. Wendy thanks her and says "you have been heard" but that sounds very unlikely.

While she switches off the white light on the screen for a minute, Wendy says please keep other questions and comments for another ten minutes as we are going to watch another recorded interview now. This one has been produced by an educational company but it was co-funded by various trusts, including ours, so we have the privilege of a preview tonight, thanks to our community programme. And then we will have the refreshments.

This second video explains conditions that can cause sight loss usually later in life, from macular degeneration to glaucoma. It makes a quick reference to Myasthenia Gravis, citing neuromuscular weakness and fatigue and other conditions that cause ptosis, eyelids drooping, change of facial expressions. For most of the time of this second presentation, I get awfully bored so I start mentally reviewing what I have to do in the coming days.

Wendy organised a reception with nibbles, fruit juices, bananas and nuts after a quick Q&A session in which nobody actually asked medical questions. There was no one that could answer them. Few non pertinent comments were elicited though, as it often happens at these meetings, about administrative issues, like when is the best time for cataract surgery or the long waiting lists for hospital appointments. It looks like some attendees came for the refreshments, and they prefer to cut the chats shortly.

Evan and I drink sparkling water and talk with another couple of presumably our age, very friendly, that I know from my local gym. She has glaucoma. He has a lazy eye, quite squinting and bulging. He remembers when he was told to do exercises with patches in primary school, like me: at that time we did not have the choice of video games. (8) I say I did exactly the same, but also for me it was too late to recuperate dioptres. We joke about the fact we might have had an accelerated training into resilience, exposing ourselves in those sort of pirates' fancy dress. Our vision did not improve, did not "return back", there was nothing to heal. Our lazy eyes remained imperturbable, before and after the occlusion of the good eyes. But we learned that in case of mysterious health issues no stone could or should remained unturned.

The man asks if I still go to the gym. Oh, yes, almost every day, I say. Physical exercise is my pain killer for arthralgia. Evan confirms that I am used to walk ten and more miles without hesitation. True, true, I say.

Tom, another man of my age I know from the gym, and his elderly mother join us. We chat about how we exercise with and without glasses or, in Tom's case, with contact lenses. His mother, who must be over 90s, says she doesn't bother to wear glasses anymore. Evan intervenes to say experts in neuroscience and neuroplasticity are promoting training that they claim can make permanent changes to the brain, including the visual cortex. The lazy eye could be re-awakened and rebalanced, without any surgery, at any age, at least according to these researchers, and no glasses as well. Oh, wow. We are all listening Evan now. The method he is referring too apparently helps with strabismus in children and even with other pathologies connected with astigmatism in adults (9).

I wonder if with all my early writing and reading in my childhood I could have made some paediatric neuroplasticity self training or, on the contrary, if I have worsened an already established amblyopia. In theory, it is not impossible to think that I have conditioned my lazy eye to adapt to some sort of neglected attention to it and stop the complete loss of vision and the squint to take over.   The aetiology of strabismus, Evan is saying, has been recently reviewed and there are four hypothesis to explain it, all compatible with the characteristics of Sjögren's, Lupus and other autoimmune diseases: genetic susceptibility, extra-ocular muscle tension, visual feedback, and eyelid pressure.

I add that according to specialists, misaligned vision from the two eyes causes not only strabismus and squint but also another symptom often seen in autoimmunity that is diplopia (double vision). The lack of perceived depth in some circumstances is a very distinctive symptom of thyroid eye disease. I cannot help to remember some tragicomic accidents I had, bumping into lamp posts I did not see coming or cars parked in an awkward position along pavements.

The old lady laughs: "You see? You see?"

Her son congratulates me for my appearance by the way: "Your eyes look much better than the last time I saw you. Have you tried any new eye drops or what is the secret?" he asks, almost seriously. I am not keen to explain, at least not here, how I take care of my eyes and sight so I opt for a vague and little amusing answer they all understand: "Ah, miracles of the Bates method", I say (10). Evan continues to entertain us for other few minutes, briefly explaining that there is a revival of Bates optometry actually. As usual, I find him quite engaging. Then Wendy materialises behind him to say that perhaps we have talked about too many different problems tonight, as astigmatism is recognised in people with so many different health conditions.

"Trying to connect its aetiology to a specific human profile is like dealing with baldness or freckles", she says, perhaps feeling the need to justify the mediocrity of the event she must be somehow aware of. "Eerybody can have them together with innumerable other diseases".

"Well, we have to go or you miss your train" I cut shortly touching Evan's elbow. We are not the only ones. Everybody seems quite happy to go home.

There is a lovely breeze for this time of the year. Evan and I walk back towards the station, where I left my bicycle. Evan returns home, in West Hampstead.

"Will you come to the walk on Sunday?" he asks, as soon we are out, passed the zebra crossing towards the park. We mentioned this forthcoming walk earlier, at the pub.

"Yes. I am so sorry we missed the ballet", I say, still regretting the choice.

Indeed, I still feel sorry we did not go to the theatre, and quite exhausted for an evening of so poorly presented information on issues so widely experienced in our neighbourhood. I am somehow in a hurry to get over it.

"I knew you would say that.", Evan laughs.

"I think I am going to call Wendy tomorrow", I say. "I want to congratulate with her for the very interesting and engaging event she

organised so efficiently. I will invite her for a cup of tea. Then I will tell her I have too many things on my mind at the moment, so…"
I do not finish the phrase. Evan does it for me: "You cannot make commitments to volunteer for the community spirit any longer".
"That's it", I say. We have a laugh.

Notes

(1) Human normal vision is called binocular single vision because the eyes form two images but the brain perceives it at a single one. It is not existing at birth: we are not born with it. It is acquired during the first four months of life and it is considered completed by the age of 6 or 7. However, still today, the development of human sight remains subject to conjectures, assumptions not always corroborated with definitive scientific evidence. What is certain is that, at birth, the eyes move randomly and there is no fixation. Then innumerable factors can interfere with the ability of the visual cortex to learn the mental processes necessary to promote and sustain binocular single vision.
According to *Moorfield Manual of Ophthalmology* (2020), astigmatism is often overestimated in children, secondary to off-axis retinoscopy, the technique used to measure the refractive error of the eye. The recommendation is to correct astigmatism equal or greater than 1.50 dioptries but it is also made clear that guidelines are to be interpreted case by case.
The Moorfield Manual warns about a great variety of complex, practical situations encountered in paediatric ophthalmology: "Amblyopia is a condition of reduced visual function, usually in one eye but sometimes in both, that is not improved by correcting any refractive error or pathological obstacle to vision (for example cataract)". A characteristic of this condition is the fact that it refers to loss of vision in one or both eyes, that is often partially reversible, and for which no actual physical cause can be found. A particular form of amblyopia is called stimulus deprivation amblyopia that specialists believe arises from the "lack of adequate visual stimulus in early life".
Up to 5 per cent of the population lacks these mechanism for combining the images from the two eyes. Why? This question has not yet received a definitive answer: "The exact brain mechanisms involved in disparity detection are still a subject of debate. The prerequisite is that there should be cells in the cortical visual areas

which receive inputs from both eyes, but which have slightly different receptive field locations in each eye. These cells will then pick up the same image features, but at different disparities. Such cells have been found in area V1, which receives nearly all the visual input to the cortex, and also in neighbouring areas V2, V3a, and V4. Whether one, all, or none of these regions contribute to the subjective appearance of the three-dimensional world around us goes to the heart of the question of how the brain produces the image we see" (see Land, M., Land, M., *The Eye: A Very Short Introduction*, Oxford University Press, 2014, p.57).

Amblyopia suddenly developing in adulthood can be due to traumas, infections, iatrogenic causes including measurement errors (off-axis retinoscopy), brain tumors or abscesses, a stroke, diabetic retinopathy or a combination of all these circumstances that induce astigmatism. This can be even worsened with the perpetuation of the wrong prescription glasses by optometrists, particularly with varifocal lenses. Specialists tend to suspect and therefore investigate amblyopia much more frequently if there is a constant unilateral strabismus. The advice is to "never delay referral for suspected squint" in particular when there is 3rd nerve palsy with pupil involvement, orbital blowout fractures, or a 4th nerve palsy with papilloedema that should be seen by neurologists at once. Also cases of diplopia with sudden onset should require urgent investigations.

In adults, the sudden onset of diplopia and strabismus is also still considered very often just a matter for cosmetic surgery that does not require further investigations, even when there are evident signs of immunocompromised processes taking over - for instance in cases of latent autoimmune diabetes, thyroid eye disease or Graves' disease. This is due to the fundamental lack of an interdisciplinary approach to autoimmunity within the healthcare system.

For the history of amblyopia mentioned here see: Sebastian, A, *A dictionary of the history of medicine*, The Parthenon Publishing Group, 1999, that reminds that "Amblyopia toxica also called nicotinic amblyopia or tobacco amblyopia was defined in the 19th Century by doctors in England and Germany, starting with William Mackenzie in 1835, with various attempts to find a cure or effective treatments. These included also a stereoscopic instrument designed to train the eye to overcome squint, developed by London ophthalmologist Claude Worth (1896-1960) around 1906". Other historical sources the story alludes here are: De Schweinitz, G. E., *The toxic amblyopias: their classification, history, symptoms, pathology, and treatment*, Philadelphia : Lea, 1896. A digital edition of this book is available through the Wellcome Collection Library; and Loudon, SE and Simonz, HJ, *The history of the treatment of amblyopia*, Strabismus, 2005, 13(2), 93–106.

(2) "Turner Syndrome is associated with both systemic and ocular disorders that may affect the outcome and safety of corneal refractive surgery. High refractive errors, strabismus, corneal abnormalities, and autoimmune disease are particularly significant" according to Moshirfar, M et al, *Turner Syndrome: Ocular Manifestations and Considerations for Corneal Refractive Surgery*, J. Clin. Med. 2022, 11, 6853.

(3) See: Wu, M., *Redefining our vision: an updated guide to the ocular immune system*, Nature Reviews Immunology, Volume 24, December 2024, 896–911; and: Forrester, JV and McMenamin, PG, *Evolution of the ocular immune system*, Eye (2025) 39:468–477.

(4) Heterophoria or latent strabismus is a condition in which the tendency of the eyes to deviate is kept latent by the faculty of fusion. Therefore, when the influence of binocular vision is removed, for any reason, the visual axis of one eye deviates away.

The perfect alignment of the two eyes is much more a theoretical idea, an ideal our perception gives for granted, more than an actual reality of the human body. In reality we all have a minimal amount of heterophoria that comes and goes, considered physiological. Asymmetries in the orbits following injuries, anomalies in the innervation of the two eyes, in the position of the macula in relation to the optical axis of the eye, or in the strength of extra ocular muscles (very common in certain autoimmune diseases) can all cause latent, intermittent or manifest squint. The same variety of manifestations is seen in uniocular or binocular diplopia (double vision).

(5) Land, M., *The Eye: A Very Short Introduction*, cit.

(6) Grierson, I., *The Eye Book*, Liverpool University Press, 2000.

(7) Miller, NP, et al, Impact of Amblyopia on the Central Nervous System, Journal of Binocular Vision and Ocular Motility, 70:4, 182-192.

(8) Fu, E, et al, *Video game treatment of amblyopia*, Survey of Ophthalmology, Volume 67, Issue 3, P830-841, May-June, 2022. New treatments explore the effectiveness of video games, while

acknowledging that poor effectiveness of the occlusion method is not just the result of lack of compliance as specialists have lamented for long time. According to recent studies in paediatric ophthalmology, "new treatment modalities under investigation follow the theory that amblyopia is a binocular process and treatment should take into account both eyes. Binocular visual stimulation through the use of dichotic classes while playing video games is the newest treatment regimen under investigation". See also: Braverman, RS, PEDIG Studies: quality healthcare and amblyopia treatment, 21 October, 2015, in AAO.ORG website, Education Section.

(9) Levi, D, *Rethinking amblyopia 2020*, Vision Research 176 (2020) 118–129. Another recent review of strabismus, Evan is referring to later in the story is: Read SA, et al, *A review of astigmatism and its possible genesis*, Clin Exp Optom. 2007 Jan;90(1):5-19.

(10) The Bates method is a controversial approach to sight correction based on relaxation and muscular exercises, developed by the ophthalmologist William H. Bates in the early 20th Century. It is still receiving some consideration by experts and patients. For an overview and links to modern optometrists' practices see: Benson, AK, *Bates Method*, Ebsco Research Starters, 2024 (online).

The Phantom Tonsils

Jean Sami was trying to relax in the cab for the next twenty minutes or so, the time to get home after her second, urgent consultation with a ear, nose and throat specialist.

On a normal summer day, she would go jogging through the park in the sunset light. But nothing has been normal for a fortnight. Beyond tiredness, she's feeling trapped into a mute body, hoping that the mind could rescue her up soon.

The driver had been instructed by Stephanie, her PA.

Less than five minutes into the journey, a phone rang into her bag. It was the red one.

Good, as she could avoid speaking. She used this dedicated line exclusively with journalists. If she hung up without saying a word they knew something would follow - a press release, or a phone call, or Stephanie would get in touch - and she did not need, nor want, to talk to them. It was a safe, effective tactic to manage enquiries, sort of a triage procedure, until now.

"Ms Sami is James Kundera of BBC Breakfast. We would like to have a word with you on this occasion. We open tomorrow with the developing story of the so called medical strategy Tiger & Schuster brought at Morbello. We have professor Gooday from Oxford University in the studio. Expert of corporate governance, he has just released a book on scandals like Enron or Lehman & Brothers. He will say that back in the 1990s and early 2000s Tony Tiger in person was advising Union Carbide when corporate lawyers were accused of bribing American and Indian officials into tampering or destroying medical evidence related to the 1984 Bhopal disaster, the consequences of which are still very active to these days. We would like to have somebody from Tiger & Schuster on the show. You know... thousands of people suffered from horrendous skin and autoimmune diseases because of the gas tragedy, many claims for compensation never went through the Courts... Ms Sami? Allegedly, it was at that time that Tiger developed this medical strategy to disguise and cover up any corporate responsibility through falsification and destruction of medical records. We've also a statement from Transparency International …. We're seeking comments from other NGO… you know, major cases of global corporate bribery…"

Jean hung up. On the other phone Stephanie had just texted: "If you do not need me I go home". She texted back: "Goodnight".
Indeed she only wanted to fly to bed,   sleep away from all the thoughts that had hijacked her voice, reach some place of peace, rest, possible recovery.
Instead ruminations kept spinning out.
What a nut that woman, Laura Kretinsky, in spite of seeming so harmless yet quite coarse at all times. She rarely spoke with Kretinsky for more than five minutes, small talks at receptions, lift encounters - and in fairness she really did not know what to think this time. Luckily, they had different clients' portfolios.
Jean wonders how they managed to employ her, who selected or wanted her at first. Back in the days, when all the press officers were vetted and recruited personally by the President,   Kretinsky would have never found a way to enter Tiger & Schuster. She had lunch with her once, accidentally, and found Kretinsky so unpleasant, arrogant, pretentious in spite of   an evident lack of taste about everything.
A woman like that in a public relator role, who eat and talk at the same time with a full mouth… But Kretinsky was not her business. She was busy with her own clients, and had so many other stuff to care for at Tiger & Schuster.
For sure, now, Laura Kretinsly was proving how inadequate and unreliable she was.
The cab driver slowed down, almost home. The red phone rang again.
"Hello Jean, is Katrin Boreingham from Pharmaceutical Hype here. We are covering your court hearing and would like to know - ah ah - what's your strategy this time around to dig Tony Tiger out of this hole…"
Jean hung up straightaway, switched off the red phone, as the driver was parking in front of her block of flats. She shared the lift with one of her neighbours.

Double locked the door, glared at the picture of her parents on the console table: a couple in their late seventies, with the scene of their beloved, serene Tuscany hills behind. They would be probably turning into their grave now, if they knew of this scandal. They had always disapproved she left a promising career in academic publishing for public relations. In a way, it is good they are not here anymore.

For a moment, she felt like she was the dead duck of the situation, the next at Tiger & Schuster that would capitulate. She had overlooked the risk of a tide coming, and for this she felt very nervous. The early signs of this story, in retrospect, seemed to her nothing else than the machiavellian manoeuvres of Chris Faulkner, Managing Director of QPR, Tiger's main competitor, and PR Agency of the year. Very clever Chris, very clever. Was she poisoned when she had a drink with him at the Award Ceremony, few days before the Court hearing? In fact, wasn't the day after that party that she started feeling a hoarse voice?

She visualised the papers headlines: "Tiger's Director Jean Sami poses as mute to avoid jail".

She took a bath, testing her ability to (at least) emit the swoosh of a whisper, even the minimal sound would have been encouraging. But no. None. Nada. Totally aphonic. She surrendered to the water, and to one of her favourite Bruckner concerts, for a good twenty minutes. Then she started repeating mentally to herself "I can't believe this", like in a trance. She collapsed on the bed, exhausted, and fallen asleep still in her bathrobe, repeating a mental ritornello, in Italian, "Gesù Gesù aiutami tu" (Jesus Jesus help me) and, in English, like in a counterpoint, "I can't believe this". Kretinsky, not her, should have lost use of her vocal cords. That was the last wish of a day of debacle.

She woke up in a desperate silence, but for that rhythmic sort of prayer coming from a distant self she was still mentally reciting since the night before (*Gesù Gesù aiutami tu, I can't believe this. Gesù Gesù aiutami tu, I can't believe this …*).

She might have dreamt about all the conversations she could not hold during the past two weeks. She had been texting and messaging frantically to Stephanie every day. Stephanie would translate those messages into phone calls and send emails to journalists. But trying to make digital versions of all the usual rebuttals she was used to handle on behalf of the President was just unworkable. She was the spokesperson of the Board. It was unconceivable she could not speak. Not to mention the fact that *scripta manent, verba volant.* In her pivotal role, as the only non family member of the Board at Tiger & Schuster, she was non supposed to put in writing anything she had to ask or say to shareholders, lawyers, and above all to an army of journalists, public relators and lobbyists, not even using WhatsApp or other trusted encrypted technologies.

For a fraction of a millisecond she smiled at herself: in the middle of a scandal like this, her friend Lilly would say that aphony was just a divine escamotage, the ingenuity of the outstanding, genial deus ex machina personality she was renowned for in the industry. Lilly was still working as science commissioning editor at Wolves, the big publishing house. They started their career together back in the day, after Uni. Lilly helped her a lot during another crisis, when she had to justify Tiger's using the Prime Minister telephone line for some embarrassing private conversations, few years ago.

The moka pot whistled and the phone trembled on the table at the same time. Wake-up Jean. Be brave once again, she tries to encourage herself to find her usual commitment to work. She still has a motto on her social media profiles saying it all: "Work hard, play hard". How ridiculous.

It was a new voice message from Stephanie: "Good morning Jean, I hope you slept well. Tiger called at 23:30, left a message. He wants to see you as first appointment this morning. I called him a moment ago to say you are not here coz you went to see another larynx specialist yesterday who recommended you to rest, and at the moment there is nothing you could do to regain voice. I explained him you have aphonia that it is a serious problem, connected to your autoimmune disease but he just shouted as usual, he does not care. Honestly, it looks he thinks you've made it up not to speak with journalists. I had to explain to him twice that you totally lost use of your vocal cords, we need to write everything and it takes time. He shouted he wants you in, as you just need to listen what he has to say about the shit at Morbello, that you get yourself out of bed and come to listen what he has to say, etcetera with the obvious fuck fuck fucking fuck.". Stephanie was trying to lightheartedly joke about the grossness of the situation, and the usual President's bad temper - that was always a good excuse for Tony to swear with everybody, but especially with women.

Stephanie is a very good PA, she thought, probably the best she has ever had, never losing her cool. She felt an awful tension gripping her muscles and nerves in the neck and shoulders, bringing back fear. Not good. She should be doing yoga and breathing exercises, not dealing with the medical strategy shit. The ritornello of the night before still resonated with her: "Gesù Gesù aiutami tu, I can't believe this".

She wiped out that sense of hopelessness and despair clouding her mind, and texted back to Stephanie, almost automatically. "Send me a cab in 25 minutes".

Then she texted again, with the plan: "Keep him busy in the meantime, bring him all the Court files - get a trolley from the legal department on the 3rd floor. Tell him I had several calls from journalists last night. Kretinsky is fishing at "The Morning Trumpet". This should distract him". She was almost sure of this, although she had not had any message or call from Mark yet.

She meant Laura Kretinsky was looking for money, spreading the Morbello shit all around. She should be sacked asap and the lawyers sent to her at once. But is was too complicated to think about this at the moment, she would deal with Kretisnky later. Let Tiger swim in his own gravy this time. She concedes to herself.

"Yup" the PA instant replied.

The idea to go to the office was actually very uncomfortable to her body, particularly to the stinging, gritty eyes. Cramps in the shoulders paired the aphony over the last few days. Stephanie brought a bigger steam humidifier and air purifier into her office, apparently they had always had one in the meeting room in the basement, used for press conferences. At first, she drunk lot of green teas and swallowed nice quarters of teaspoons of honey, and even attempted to joke about her aphony, handing over "post it" notes to everybody, because she lost her voice suddenly, as soon as she left the the Court, after the hearing. But on the third day all the jokes and fun were gone. The voice did not return the day after, and the day after, and the day after. Perhaps it was late when she run into the clinic? Or she should avoided Dr Jones? Fact is, they hold 70% of the shares at Pembrook Diagnostics and Care and there are huge incentives to go there, for everything, for everybody. She was seen by this fat ENT specialist, doctor Jones, a couple of hours after she phoned him: in fairness, he had been brilliant few years earlier explaining her weird ear pressure problem and temporomandibular joint disorder.

Staring from a moment out of the balcony to the remote trees in the park, away from the geraniums she hasn't watered for days, and her cleaner is not bothered to care for, Jean gleans from BBC News on the Radio that Tiger & Schuster is still in the main headlines today, oh dear., but she feels her mind is now flying miles away, like a healthy sense of detachment, eventually, is taking over. Not her problem.

The repulsive face of Dr Jones visualises in front of her, interfering with the mirror while she attempts to put on some make up.

"You are lucky Ms Sami - he pronounced solemnly. - Even if the situation seems very serious, your airways are clear, no swelling in the neck nor in the tonsils, your nose is remarkably clear. Airways annoyances are common in Sjögren's disease as you know and there may be even further complications, but I do not see any reason for concern in your case at the moment. You just need to have patience, rest, take it easy, it's one of those Sjögren's things, and I am confident that your voice will be back soon".

She tried, in vain, to attract his attention on a yellow post-it sticker she had frighteningly written down while he was speaking, and showed to him: "I DO NOT HAVE THE TONSILS.". He just laughed for a moment and went on speaking, looking at his computer screen, before handing her a prescription for a mouthwash. "Yours is very likely a temporary, severe case of dysphonia, Ms Sami. Probably caused by excessive thickness of the mucosa on the vocal folds, in connection with nerves impulses. It's like a strain in a joint that makes you unable to move a limb for a few days. When it happens in the larynx, a similar dysfunctional mechanism makes the vocal fold's tiny layers of tissue, the muscles, the cartilages, the ligaments, their internal and external membranes like they were all glued together - and it can last for an hour or for weeks. You do not worry, try to relax, do your yoga and breathing exercises, keep breathing deeply if you feel any pain or spam, relax the muscles in the upper body, keep drinking sips of warm liquids, not too hot, do plenty of rinses with these medications, you need plenty of moisture, the steam humidifier as your PA told me is an excellent idea".

He looked at her and continued to laugh. "Yes, yes Ms Sami, I know. You do not have the tonsils anymore but" - and he hinted at the computer screen laughing at it with his mouth open - "we have the records from your GP that say you do have them and they are inflamed, ah ah ah".

He had a gold tooth that Jean had not seen before.

She had wanted to write another post-it to him, to say she has not been seen by her NHS GP for ages, but then she just felt an instant repulsion for Dr Jones, and his filthy allegations, and a sense of distrust prevailed over any reflection on what he had said. She just wanted to leave that damned clinic at once. Pembrook was the first private clinic Tiger & Schuster acquired. Its Board of directors was under their control. Strategic interlocks. Tiger was used to recommend all their customers they had to send employees to Pembrook for regular annual health check-ups. Pembrook was one of the most exclusive private clinics in the whole Country, so a free and thorough health check-up was seen as a huge bonus for employees.

Jean decided she had to talk with someone else, outside Tiger's circles.

Stephanie arranged for her to go to another private hospital yesterday, after a long series of unanswered email and unsuccessful phone calls to all the private ENT specialists in town: "You are lucky. Dr Katara is an emeritus professor of Otolaryngology, Neurolaryngology and Head and Neck Surgery. - She had eventually texted, in triumph. - His medical secretary said he has a very busy day but he will delay his mother-in law dinner party to see you before leaving office".

Dr Katara looked into her throat with kindness, on top of medical caution, moving in a sort of slo-mo sequence. He appreciated Joan's little post-it messages. He asked if it happened she had completely lost her voice before (she wrote on a post-it: "NO"), and if she ever suffered of episodes of laryngitis, or tracheitis, or frequent tonsillitis before the tonsillectomy she probably had as a child (he noticed she did not have the tonsils, thank Goddess!).

She replied holding the same post-it message: "YES YES YES".

She would have also liked to add that tonsillitis was an excruciating problem in her childhood, and had so many instances of weird disturbances to her throat and airways during her adolescence. But it was too long to write, and actually redundant. She just wrote on another post-it "frequent sore throat, coughing, airways inflamed in my teens and 20s".

When she started work, in a very dusty office, coughing for hours without a reason was her despair, as she was trying to get along nicely with colleagues. Then she changed job and moved to another office building, much more airy and the problem disappeared, so she forgot it. Perhaps, the very reason why she left academic publishing for corporate affairs was the better office environment.

Dr Katara spoke with great confidence, calmly and softly to explain there was no damage to her vocal cords but further assessment - namely, a laryngeal electromyography - could be needed if her voice did not come back within few days ("let's say within max another week from today"): the nerves into the larynx can be very easily injured, he said, because they are connected with neck and chest through the so called recurrent nerve: "it is called recurrent exactly because it goes up and down and all around the neck, and it is exposed to all sorts of micro traumas. We do not think about it but these minimal and yet disabling traumas can happen to the nerves, everywhere in the body, at any time. Even a big meal can upset the recurrent nerve for days (1).

Jean thought Dr Katara was encouraging. He said her voice could very likely come back without any medication, on its own, and this might have happened anytime, out of the blue exactly as it had vanished last week, after the Court hearing. Perhaps he was aware of the developing scandal at Tiger's since he added that "sometimes a reaction to stress in autoimmune diseases can take the form of a temporary impairment"?

Don't get paranoid, she implored herself, thinking back to this second consultation while dressing, as the cab would arrive in minutes and she still had to eat breakfast.

She had to admit she did not learn anything fundamentally different from Dr Jones's diagnosis and prognosis after seeing Dr Katara, but she was reassured and felt less anxious. She appreciated a very different way to talk about the problem. Plus, Dr Katara gave her a business card with a mobile number, and pat her shoulder while escorting her to the lift, reassuring her he would be available for emergencies: "Many cases I have seen in anatomy and physiology of the voice taught me that the best initial medicine with these issues is patience. Do please text me if there is any further symptom, like pain anywhere in the neck or chest, but above all do not worry. It's unlikely you have any serious problem with your voice".

During the visit he also mentioned the hypothesis that her aphonia could have been caused by some chemicals she had accidentally breathed ("sometimes a fragile immune system can overreact to what would be otherwise a light, temporary irritation. In doing so, the body is perpetuating or escalating a sort of allergic reaction, up to the point that the vocal cords need to shut down in self-defence"). However, there was no actual certainty: "Vocal folds dysfunctions are on the rise also in the normal population, not only among people with Sjögren's... pollution, indoor particulate matters... there are many volatile substances that we do not even know we breathe, and they are very harmful to us in a way or another".

Jane tried to remember all the occasions in which she could have been exposed to volatile chemicals. Perhaps that was exactly what happened when she had her tonsils removed? for causes that were very contingent to the building work that was ongoing in their big house at that time.   She got her tonsillectomy because her parents were advised that was the best course of action but ...who knows. Two small masses of constantly inflamed lymphoid tissue in the throat, her poor tonsils could have been seen as a warning about the susceptibility of her glands and lymph nodes to become attacked by an autoimmune mechanism, mistaking volatile chemicals that are innocuous to many for dangerous allergens. Fact is, there was no such attention to autoimmunity in the late 1960s. Few years later she lost in similar urgent circumstances the gallbladder, the appendix, and also a molar with a big granuloma in her jaw, all requiring emergency surgery in total anaesthesia.   The removal of her tonsils was just recommended to avoid risks of complications due to her frequent infections. Those two minimal lymphoid organs went gone in minutes, as far as she can remember, and then she was offered ice-cream for days.

At the time of Jean's tonsillectomy, around the age of 10, losing them was seen as normal (2). Now things are different. Nowadays there are more choices of treatment, she read some time ago somewhere, and doctors do not rush parents to proceed with surgery. That seems a very sensible choice. Once the not so "non vital" little organs are gone... they are gone forever. Perhaps her vocal cords remember the time she had her two tonsils in place?   The tonsils could have performed additional, minimal yet helpful protective tasks in her body in this awful circumstance, if only they had been in place... Come on, Jean, get ready, go out.... The phantom tonsils sensing how much of an idiot was Kretinsky? Filtering out volatile chemicals in the Court room? Well… who knows.

Perhaps the occasional sore throats, the mildly swollen lymph nodes in the neck, the larynx irritated by air conditioning system and so on and so forth are all problems she could have prevented and avoided, if only she had kept her tonsils! (3)

The phone vibrated on the table, flushing away her mulling over the fatigued interactions she had been having for the last few days. The cab was waiting for her downstairs, Stephanie texted.

She swallowed the last sip of coffee at once and grabbed the pouch with the toothbrush and mouthwash from the kitchen counter.

As soon as she sat down in the car and switched it on, the red phone started ringing and notifications of various texts messages flashed on the screen.

"Jean, good morning. Mark Lynch here. I have heard from your office you have been unwell. I am sorry, let me know if … when we can talk … After last week I can imagine it must be a tough time…"

"Hmm" she struggled to make any sound at all, but Mark was almost a friend, and she would have really liked to speak with him this time, if only she could. His tone was genuinely scared.

"We should talk Jean, as soon as possible as we have a big piece coming up. I have been asked to work it out. This thing is spreading rapidly Jean. Borg put a trainee on the Court papers, and this girl, Adele Short her name - perhaps rings a bell - managed to interview Laura Kretinsky. It is a long tape, full of details, names, years… Borg says there is material for a podcast and he wants it on the first page of 'The Morning Trumpet' tomorrow… Kretinsky's version is that she is being treating as a scapegoat, because Tiger & Schuster had a long standing way to blackmail employees and even consultants on behalf of all the clients they audited, not just at Morbello… that the medical strategy was the cover up for a network of systemic corruption… that trading medical records was seen as perfectly normal… in sum a huge scandal Jean… by way of mingling with doctors, bribing nurses and administrators, tampering personal data… Jean this is huge, you know … accessing private health data, even insurance claims … Kretinsky says this has been going on for a very long time, with all the members of the board secretly knowing what the medical strategy was all about, not just check-ups and well-being programmes offered to employees but actual a way to kill whistleblowers, to keep people quiet... Please call back ... tell me if you are going to send a statement, or you want to comment ... It is almost unbelievable that Tiger succeeded to keep so many people quiet for so long .... also all the acquisitions Tiger made in the healthcare and life sciences sector over the last twenty years, these are going to be reviewed and considered in a new light... you know ...what should be done? everything seems now into Kretinsky basket ...   Jean - Mark's tone was almost imploring her - we need to talk, this is not usual stuff... it is a massive sinister story ... Jean? Please answer the....".

She hung up on him and put the red phone on silent, swallowing little saliva and taking a long breath in. And read a message on the other phone.

"Good morning Jean. - It was from her friend Lilly. "I just had a chat with Stephanie, I wanted to say how sorry I am Jean, it must be an agony to have aphony... (smiley) it really does strikes a CORD with me, ah ah, excuse the pun (smiley) You let me know, alright? anything I can I will do it for you".

Then was another text from Stephanie, including a video message this time, showing just a slice of her face while she was pushing the trolley she got from the 3rd floor with the left hand and holding the phone with the right, towards the lift, slightly panicking, but still somehow in control of her usual sense of humour: "He has just phoned again Jean. asking if you have arrived. I told him you are in the cab and I am on my way to his office right now with the documents you ask him to see and you will be here in minutes".

In a split second decision Jean texts back, with no need to ponder anything further: "I am not coming. I leave. He will receive my resignation letter by the end of the day, tomorrow at the latest. Health reasons. Tell him I amicably recommend him to read all those files you are bringing to him with the lawyers. Tell him you are happy to remain at Tiger in any other suitable position. Then go home. Call Lilly from your landline. Tell her I got her message and I would like her to help you find a better place to work. I am going to text her now I resigned, so she will know. I will stay abroad for a couple of weeks. I am going to visit my parents' grave in Tuscany. I will call both of you as soon as my voice is back. Best of luck. Stephanie, thank you very much for your extraordinary support and assistance over many years. We will talk again".

Then she texts Lilly with her big news.

She reached into the bag to find the post-it block and a pen to write the message for the driver, but while she messed around all the stuff in the bag, she heard herself almost shouting: "STOP PLEASE, STOP. GO BACK TO MY HOUSE PLEASE".

The driver looked at her in the rear-view mirror, disconcerted: she was mute minutes earlier, now she was shouting.

"Do you want to go back to your house, to your house where I picked you up?" the taxi driver raised his voice too.

Jean was laughing and crying at the same time: "Yes yes, please. I can talk, my voice is back. I can talk!" She almost shouted again.

And she laughed, and she cried too.

Notes

(1) *Anatomy and physiology of the voice*, in Laryngeal Electromyography, 3rd ed., Plural publishing, 2017, p. 11, explains that the soft tissues lining the larynx are made of different molecular structures: inflammation in this part of the body causes a wide range of conditions. Medical literature often describes the lining of the larynx detailing up to three or five layers. The mucosa forms a thin, lubricated surface around the vocal cords that are in contact with each other when the glottis closes. Such mucosa consists of goblet cells, seromucinous glands, and squamous epithelium for the production and handling of mucous secretions, similarly to the mucosa existing in the rest of the respiratory tract but with peculiar features due to the fact that the vocal cords are in constant contact, friction, mobilisation. The recurrent laryngeal nerve (RLN) and the superior laryngeal nerve (SLN) are branches of cranial nerve X, or vagus nerve. The innervation of the larynx may also supply motor and sensory innervation to the vocal cords. A characteristic of the anatomy and physiology of this part of the body is that not two individuals have identical number and position of laryngeal nerves and motor fibres. This means infinite variations in the way in which the vagus nerve and vagal reflexes interact with the vocal cords are possible. This combinatory variety affects also the muscles that move the vocal folds. Similarly, there is great variability in the diameter of the fiber distribution of laryngeal muscles compared to other muscles in the body.

(2) Like the lymph nodes in the neck, groin and armpits, the tonsils are make of lymphoid tissue but since they are impacted by breathing and eating, they can be infected more frequently and easily than other lymph nodes in the body. In medical literature, tonsils are often described as the "filter for the lymphatic system", a metaphor that translates very well their important   function that decreases as we grow older. Perhaps for this last reason, for long time the medical community believed the tonsils were not very important for human health. Medical textbooks still state that the palatine tonsils and their adenoid (or pharyngeal tonsils - the ones located at the back of the throat) can be removed in children without any loss of immunity because, as reported in A McDowell, J. and Windelspecht, M., *The lymphatic system*, Westport - London, Greenwood Press, 2004, there is a widespread belief that "the body has redundant systems lined up such as other lymph nodules, that will serve the same function if the tonsils are removed". Such belief had been disputed and criticised since long by thyroid experts like Dr Barry Durrant-Peatfield.

(3) Current medical protocols are more cautious than in recent past, and recommend tonsillectomy according to the number of tonsils' infections a child experiences in a given period of time: in this way clinical guidance has drawn a line between the pros and cons of keeping them: "Tonsillectomy should be reserved for recurrent peritonsillar abscesses and should only take place following the resolution of infection" I read in *Head and Neck, Tonsils*, StatPearls (Internet), July 17, 2023. Also, it seems nowadays accepted that a child can develop Juvenile Sjögren's following tonsillectomy: Scientists have ascertained there is an association between tonsillectomy and the development of Sjögren's or an increased disease activity - and the same seems true in cases of appendectomy according to Kollert, F. et al., *History of tonsillectomy is associated with glandular inflammation in Sjögren's disease*, Rheumatology, 61, 7, July 2022, e168-170. For these reasons, the removal of the tonsils is not something doctors would rash to recommend anymore, before trying other treatments, especially if there is a suspect of a genetic susceptibility or a family history of autoimmune diseases.

A Casual Lymph

Adolescence arrived as a typhoon. The doctor explained to her mother that Vera did not have any pelvic floor muscle dysfunction. Nor she suffered from cysts, malformations, pressure on the nerves. So she could not be diagnosed at the age of 10 with any persistent genital arousal disorder (1). "It's just nature", he said.

The family doctor was unable to explain why Vera was having abnormal vaginal lubrication at that very young age, and in all sorts of embarrassing situations. The girl explained the monstrous discharge was happening at school, and every time she came back home after playing with her male classmates and neighbours Alan and Henry, and even during night time. There was no concomitant sexual arousal at all, at first. Vera feared she might have weed in her pants without feeling any urgency to go to the bathroom. How strange.

Eventually, things started to settle and look consequential, at least to her. Vera was in awe: in life, like in maths or grammar, there are hidden, self-explaining rules, not always clear to doctors, nor parents.

She kept asking questions about forces and fears, wonder and mysteries that were battling in her body. Not that answers would make any difference, but it would have been nice to know why. Answers were always quite scarce. Sometimes there were none, as her parents were busy fighting each other before the divorce.

Vera's mother had little patience: "Why, why, why.... Ask you dad.", she would say quite often, and send her away.

Perhaps the menarche interrupted her childhood too soon, causing pelvic and abdominal spams for a couple of years - and even more questions.

"Congratulations. And don't worry", laughed her father, informed by mum that Vera had become "Miss Vera", menstruating every month, like a woman, at that young age.

***

It's almost unbelievable to think she has now lost her libido, at the age of 38, with the perimenopause in theory still further down the line. The reason? Hard to say. Boredom? Other priorities? Stress? Once every two or three years she happens to look at a man with that type of sexual attention, but she has so many other things to do and to think. She has just lost interest in sex.

"Your thyroid is normal, in spite of high levels of antibodies attacking it, but hypothyroidism develops subtly and slowly over time", told her the last endocrinologist she spoke with, so that he concluded: "we need to stay vigilant". How, she would have liked to know.

It can be luckier playing bingo than saying with certainty the cause of loss of libido is a malfunctioning thyroid, especially when the level of thyroid hormone is normal, and there is any overt menopausal hormonal imbalance (2).

Borderline or subclinical hypothyroidism can be difficult to prove with lab tests, being the exact point of imbalance very different for each person. In every woman, sexual hormones make a unique mix and match we can barely try to figure out with all the lab tests. Even if you fall in what is considered statistically the normal range, it may be that your thyroid produces levels of one hormone too low for your wellbeing, and that's it. The same is true with auto-antibodies: minimal amount of these can cause great systemic havoc in some while high values are perfectly well tolerated in others.

Diagnosis of thyroid and autoimmune diseases is controversial and difficult for these reasons. Another endocrinologist said the quantity of antibodies detected in her blood was enough to explain why she has lost any sexual drive: she had Hashimoto's thyroiditis. Her rheumatologist disagreed: she had "only" fibromyalgia and Sjögren's, being her thyroid perfectly normal.

Opening the pouch with her packed lunch she swore in her mind at the consultants (*fuck you all!*). What a huge waste of time, money, quality of life trying to understand what's going on in her body according to standards.

***

She is going to Penzance, for a job on the west coast. Somebody from the team of archeologists she is going to work with will come to pick her up. She is sleeping in a B&B next to the campsite, along the coastal path. It must be very nice indeed during the summer.

Her contract is for just one month: she will act as Fixed Term Finds Manager on the campsite, but they may need to call her back again in few months time, fingers crossed, as she needs more work.

For now, one month is enough. They pay the lowest possible rate. She agreed with the Principal investigator she would catalogue everything from the dig they already have, prepare and send the materials for specialist assessment, and that's it. This will prevent the backlog to become totally unmanageable. In the meantime they will try to get more funding.

As soon as the train leaves London Paddington, crowded as it is always on Fridays afternoons, she can eventually relax and have her packed dinner: a sandwich with gluten free flatbread she makes herself, filled with an omelette cooked in the oven - so there is no need to fry anything. She mixes eggs with boiled asparagus and herbs or courgettes, plus a couple of spoons of fat free yogurt, and a minuscule quantity of butter for the silicon dish - like 10 grams or less. She makes this type of sandwich occasionally, once or twice a month. Sometimes with rice cakes instead of the flatbread, usually for a picnic.

A handsome gentleman in the opposite seat kind of stares at her with an inquisitive smile while she eats with evident smugness.

Vera thinks she may exhibit an excess of delight, eating that rare, better say unique, delicatessen. All in all, it is embarrassing, though. It is seriously impolite to stare others while they are eating with appetite.

She sips some water from her bottle, still fresh, pretending she did not notice him. But the guy goes on. Does he find me funny? Is my appetite contagious?, she thinks it is quite annoying to be watched. But perhaps she is overreacting.

The man looks amused, he may be just curious.

Vera does not want to speak, nor to be seduced, nor to get rid of the earphones. So she finishes the water and the green tea and then just looks out of the window, listening to the music.

***

Passed the Greater London boundary, the sunset looks beautiful.

Another train journey comes to mind, with another man staring at her eating, when she met Victor. It was at the beginning of her career. Another handsome young man, another casual encounter, another time.

She had the fortune to be chosen for an internship that was all she had to do for her degree thesis. Victor was fatal attraction at first sight, back then.

He was seating in front of her, smiling sweetly, while she was eating her packed dinner. The three hours train journey would take her to a camp accommodation in East Anglia, where she would sleep in a tent with other two students. After a good sleep, they would have a big breakfast next to the dig, and then attend the briefing meeting with excavation experts and a professor. It was such an adventurous career, and she felt so lucky to be chosen for that assignment.

They would work during the day, then go out with the archeologists' team in the evening, drink and eat at the pub with other students coming from other universities, for a week. The next Sunday evening she would return back to London, back to her part-time job at the museum, and all her usual routines. She had agreed with colleagues she would work all her due hours in three weeks instead of four so that she could have one week per month totally devoted to her University degree in Archeology.

The deputy director, a short fat woman that she heard calling her "that black tart" once, had something to say about the arrangement. However the complaint was easily dumped down by the director, an elegant Irish lady close to retirement who did not find anything wrong with Vera's schedule: after all, she was employed because she was doing that degree, and started her career as an apprentice. The director was so pleased with Vera's academic ambitions ,and willingness to experiment life on the campsite. So that she did not find worthwhile to waste time to stop colleagues' gossiping about her or the deputy director's slander.

***

Victor was staring at her in silence. That lasted a long, long time, perhaps half the journey, but in a way that was unequivocally sexy. Vera liked him very much, but for a while she did not want to talk with him, as she was just resting and cradling herself, thinking about something ahead in her work-student balance for that week. It was only after the train passed Norwich that she returned a smile, and looked into his eyes. Victor did not say a word, clearly signalling he preferred to leave to her any initiative.

"You on levies?" Vera asked eventually.

"Yes", he smiled more. She was on his hook, at last: "How did you know?"

"I do this journey every three weeks, approximately every month, for my University degree". She explained her double life, sort of.

He introduced himself with pride, being a pilot and paratrooper trainee. He was thinking of joining the army as a professional parachutist. They kept talking and staring at each other in a silence full of reciprocal curiosity, and desire, for a couple of hours at least, until the train approached his stop, that was the station nearest to his military base, just 20 minutes ahead of hers. He wrote a phone number on a scrapped piece of newspaper in a hurry, when he was just about to get off the train. "Call me, ask to speak with me", he implored her. He said he would have free time on the following Tuesday evening, and he would come to see her as soon as his shift was over, after 3pm.

The idea was so enticing. "I will think of it", she said, with a scent of vanity and a smile that promised more, much more.

She was experiencing one of her seasons of extraordinary, if not dysfunctional, libido. Would have made any difference if she had met Victor at another time, or in another situation? She wonders now.

***

There were times in her youth in which she would have liked to have sex three or more times a day. It wasn't something right or wrong, nor it was anything in any way connected with love, or expectations of a relationship or the like. Nothing like that.

It was just a mad drive for sexual gratification, to let sexual arousal and orgasms flood her skin.

An unstoppable desire of touching, holding, kissing, fusing and melting with another body was overwhelmingly occupying most of her thoughts and feelings for days, mixing with everything she wanted or had to do, undoubtedly confusing, or altering, her priorities and choices especially after work and when she had free time from Uni.

As a young woman, she could not openly joke about her sexual appetite, like men often do without fear of being accused of priapism, toxic masculinity or perversions (3).

For men, it is almost normal to socially disclose they have a sort of strong vigour, an urgent sexual drive, as long as their behaviour does not give rise to complaints of misconduct, or embarrassment due to total inappropriateness.

Vera learned in her teens that too much disclosure of her sexual appetite, for just the fact of being female, could be judged as reprehensible and invade any other space of her life, no matter the fact that was decent and well managed. Some girls she knew - classmates, then colleagues at work - were covertly going out with two or three men at the same time, for the sake of testing them somehow and gossiping about it, but always carefully keeping it as a secret.

Conversely, for few years in the high school and then when she started work, Vera did not care too much about people judgements: with a working class background, and the aspiration to become an archeologist, she was prepared to be seen in a suspicious light by some. Year after year, the fact she remained single, and she was having affairs without being engaged with anybody, was rumoured in a strange way, somehow despicable, leaving her without options to defend her reputation, or firing back. Somebody even said around she was homosexual. Being very much straight and deeply in love with the idea of making love with men, that falsehood about her identity really offended her.

Did her libido drown into self-censorship? did she cause herself more harm than good, ignoring all the nasty word of mouth she was targeted with for years, allowing to dig a hole for herself?

She could not reveal her sexual appetite openly, to avoid dozens of female eyes on her. Repercussions of her affairs sometimes rippled at work, making the deputy director and other women very hostile to her without a reason. Her mother would then call to ask her who she was going out with this time around, that she inevitably thought should deserve a guillotine being too old for her or too married.

Most rumours were obviously triggered by her disinhibited choice of casual partners: deluded married men, escapists, divorcees. And with Victor, even the military. But almost every story of that portfolio of relationships without a future other than casual sex was actually quite sweet. She finds lovely and tender to remember she liked her lovers.

***

Why had her nature turned into a total loss of libido now? Sometimes she thinks that she has had an interrupted existence as a human being, without a reason. She would not say that as a child she was maltreated, or that she totally lacked parental affection.

Rather, she was chronically left behind, praised in public and unsupported or even diminished in private. In that toing and froing of parental attention, she learned to grow up caring for herself as much as she could. Her emotional and sensory development was a swing, sometimes she would stay hours almost still, in a frozen state of fear, waiting for her mum to come back from a spell of depression or just open the door of the garage where she had locked her in for some reason. At other times, she would be able to fly higher and higher compared to her classmates, and really be the champion, the distinguished child that adults would praise for their behaviour, intelligence, or creativity. She would not say she was fishing for compliments, approval, validation of any sort.

However, seducing older boys and young men in those moments of intense, premature arousal became indeed an exercise in self-sooting, a reassuring yet impulsive behaviour that took a very long time to decipher, being so intertwined with the need to be loved and cared for. Dating men for sexual relationships would modulate her emotions according to some healthy rule of its own, not depending on anything else other than an inner call of the body.

In a certain sense, the disruptive power of sex was a space for Vera to have agency in her life, where her mother would not be allowed to enter, nor to lock any door: she simply would not dare, could not play any part in those type of things.

Vera became quickly aware that her sexual power had some drawbacks though: she was at risk of falling victim of predatory adults, cheaters, emotionally unresponsive men or even perverts.

In any case, thinking of having a stable, conventional relationship with most of the boys and men she dated in her teens and 20s would have been totally preposterous. Nevertheless, from time to time, romance would take over: she would dream, may be for just one day or one week, a forever future together with someone, thanks to the intensity of some special physical or intellectual attraction. That was exactly what happened with Victor.

***

She did phoned him the day after that encounter on the train.

They agreed for Tuesday evening. She went to meet him at the station, they spent the night above the pub next to the campsite. She was happy she could say to her mates: "My boyfriend is coming to see me and we are staying together tonight". There was no need to say she did not know anything about him but his name and his role in the nearby RAF base.

Victor's body was amazing, the dream of any young woman who is fantasising about sex and romance. He was a truly exceptional lover too, the one that gives you a world of tenderness hugging you and radiates irresistible sexual energy just holding your hand.

Kind and strong, Victor would not leave an inch of her skin untouched. He would kiss her everywhere.

The only detail she was not happy to call to mind, the visual memory of which annoyed her now, twenty years on, is that they were both heavy smokers.

She is now allergic to smoke and wonders how could they make to smoke all those cigarettes in one night. Blame youth. It was another age, other bodies.

After sex they would smoke one of Victor's cigarettes together in silence, staring at the ceiling of their essential but charming countryside bedroom, chatting aloud with the window open, the spring breeze from the sea feeling silky on her naked legs.

It went on for a couple of months. They went on meeting on trains, kissing each other passionately on platforms, running to the pub's bedroom once or twice when Vera was at the campsite, one week per month.

Eventually the summer arrived and pulled the plug on their passion.

Victor knew she would not go to the campsite during the summer months because all the University work would be suspended. He announced he would come to see her in London.

It was somehow unexpected, but she had not prepared any excuse so she said yes. It seemed obvious that they both wanted to see each other during the summer too.

She remembers the reluctance she felt at first, a certain sense that an inevitable end should be coming anyhow. She knew she had to manage that ending stage, in spite of the sexual attraction and the sense of peace she felt in Victor's company.

Perhaps there was something fundamentally wrong with her, with her libido tantrums, with her fear - yes, it was fear - of a relationship not ending in the morning.

Perhaps she had just run out of excuses to truncate that story, and the anxiety was mounting. Her mother and sister would go away for three weeks on holiday. Vera had to go to work, at least until mid August. So all in all, Victor's idea seemed easy. They could indeed organise something in London too.

He caressed her groin and thighs and asked with apprehension: "What are these lymph nodes?"

"Hmmmm? Interested?", she joked, genuinely not understanding what he meant, if he had something nice in mind or what else.

"I mean, they seem swollen", he said, very serious.

She pretended she did not catch his apprehension, and that everything was fine.

"You remind me my mum" Vera laughed, releasing tension. "When I was little she was used to check my lymph nodes from time to time. I had to lie down on the bed, and show her my groin so that she could inspect if the lymph nodes were normal or bigger than they should. It was like going to the gynaecologist!", Vera showed off the emotional detachment she had learned to impose to herself by that age, whenever she remembered something of her childhood of swollen lymph nodes and premature, abnormal vaginal lubrication.

"So... you have been having these swollen lymph nodes for a long time?" the young man asked, even more worried, with no sign of amusement at all in his mesmerising blue eyes.

Whatever the thrill, it had gone in those few instants.

"Oh yes. What's worrying you?" Vera was now irritated. Now she really wanted to know.

"Nothing, it's just unusual... but if you know that everything is ok with your lymph nodes there is no problem".

"What should be not ok? What are you talking about?" Vera insisted, almost willing to forgive him for ruining their post-sex romantic atmosphere, the last night of their season of passion.

She would have liked to look into his sexy and tender eyes, forever. She was prepared to forgive him for having cut shortly that feeble, timid attempt she was secretly trying, or hoping to be able to try, to imagine they would go ahead and see each other again, and again, and again. Instead, it was clear there would not be a beginning of something with Victor.

She felt that would be impossible to see him again. But she liked him, and liked his body very much. It was an instant of death that took over deeply inside, when she realised they did not have any future.

"My mum died of lymphoma" Victor said, blowing softly on her shoulder, turning on his side to gently kiss her neck.

Everything was over in seconds.

"Never heard of it" she said, just retracting a bit. She wanted to get dressed soon.

"It's a cancer of the lymphatic system", Victor said exhaling smoke.

***

Vera pretended she was not impressed, using a childish voice, while quickly grabbing her bra and pants, going to the bathroom: "You are scaring me", she laughed.

It was awful to admit it, but truth was she did not want to see him anymore.

She had those little bubbles swelling under the skin of the groin for several years as a teenager. They were not painful so she could not remember they were a particular concern, although some lymph nodes were uncomfortable under the tights or the trousers. It was like walking with a little stone in the shoes. It wasn't nice to notice them when she stayed long hours in her swim costume, or wearing a biking on the beach. But season after season, month after month after month the unusually big lymph nodes became something confirming her identity, neither to be worried about nor to keep under medical observation. It was just something peculiar to her.

However, at some point, mother decided they had to ask the doctor what was the cause of that strange swelling. The doctor confirmed the cherry plums under the skin were swollen, inflamed lymph nodes: the cause might have been rheumatisms, or iron deficiency, or some other unknown cause in connection with her hormonal development. So he advised to be vigilant, and to come back for more investigations if the lymph nodes became suddenly bigger.

What she would have liked both her and her mother knew at that time was that her body was struggling to accommodate the demand of an unusual lymphatic system while she was growing up: she needed more space perhaps, physically and mentally, less emotional and material interruptions to her teenager life, a calmer family life, surely less tensions affecting all her glands.

Growing up, her swollen lymph nodes in the groin disappeared or considerably shrunk although some were still palpable under the skin in her early twenties, especially during the summer months.

Victor might have noticed them because they were still the size of garden peas at that time. By the age of 40 they became almost unnoticeable, although still sweating unusually hard from time to time.

***

The man in front of her is collecting his two pieces of luggage from the upper rack: he's going off at Exeter St David. He says something to the woman seated next to him. Vera does not catch what. She does not need to hurry up.

"Madam, Madam, the train divides here, are you in the correct part of the train?", asks a conductor.

Yes, she was. Vera is thinking her life has been interrupted so many times.

Nobody knows what the true causes of autoimmune diseases, and hypothyroidism, and Sjögren's, and Myasthenia Gravis or Thyroid Eye Disease are. There isn't a single cause. But so many interruptions happened in her young life, and made her who she is today, with all her shrunken lymph nodes and gluten free home made sandwiches.

"Madam where are you heading towards?" the train guard asks again, nervous.

"Oh sorry" she realises she is still on her own train of thoughts. "I am going to Penzance", she smiles to the fat man.

"Yes, Madam this coach goes to your final destination. You are travelling in the correct part of the train"

Her two companions leave the coach instead.

"Enjoy the rest of your journey" the handsome man says. It looks like he would have liked to have a chat.

"The same to you", Vera replies, smiling.

It feels a smile back to the future.

Notes

(1) After several years of medical debates, in 2019 a consensus was reached to define a Persistent Sexual Arousal Disorder (PSAD), also known as Persistent Genital Arousal Disorder (PGAD), as a condition affecting sexual health. As such PSAD/PGAD is now classified in the 11th edition of the International Classification of Diseases, (ICD-11) published in 2022 and deemed to come into implementation by 2027 with a more holistic model of female sexual activity. In particular, experts have highlighted that is now superseded the dualistic idea of dividing pathological states on the grounds of biological / physical and psychological / mental aetiology. On the contrary, female sexual dysfunction is now seen as result of complex interactions of many factors (psychological, interpersonal, social, cultural, physiological, gender identity).

Within the World Health Organisation ICD-11, the diagnostic criteria for compulsive sexual behaviour disorder or CSBD still exist, allowing to make clear distinctions among different types of apparently similar behavioural patterns that impact sexual health and development. CSBD characteristics include a distinctive "pattern of failure to control intense, sexual impulses or urges and resulting repetitive sexual behaviour" that must be manifested over an extended period of time, for instance six months or more, causing "marked distress or significant impairment in personal, family, social, educational, occupational or other important areas of functioning". With such definitions experts wanted to rule out as a criterion for diagnosis the recognition of a state of "distress" that can be very common and totally obvious in a wide range of healthy and unhealthy individuals and above all it "is entirely related to moral judgements and disapproval about sexual impulses, urges or behaviours" and not of any medical interest.

(2) The loss of libido in connection with autoimmune diseases and thyroid dysfunctions, in particular Hashimoto's thyroiditis and hypothyroidism, is discussed in many textbooks and research articles published during the last twenty years. According to the late Dr Barry Durrant-Peatfield, renowned for his great expertise about thyroid diseases, a low thyroid state (hypothyroidism) affects the onset of the menarche that may come unusually early (between 8 and 10 years of

age) with some consequentiality to tonsillectomy. The menstruation of girls affected by hidden, subclinical hypothyroidism after the menarche may be abnormal in other ways, such as excess pain, collapse or prostration, facial pallor or orbital edema, irregular pulse rate, intolerances to cold and heat. Connecting signs and symptoms of glands dysfunctions in the whole body, both exocrine and endocrine, Dr Durrant-Peatfield notes that in patients with subclinical hypothyroidism, often under-diagnosed for many years, loss of libido, headaches, poor resistance to infections, arthralgia and a perimenopause state of hormonal fluctuations and imbalances (in particular, DHEA or dehydroepiandrosterone) may start in the late 30s and early 40s. A group of disorders called autoimmune polyglandular syndromes causes autoimmune diseases that attack the thyroid as well as the adrenals and other glands and soft tissues. See: Durrant-Peatfield, B., *Your Thyroid and how to keep it healthy. Second edition of The Great Thyroid Scandal and how to Survive it*, London, Hammersmith Press, 2007, p. 50.

"Sjögren's can affect women's sexual function" writes Anne E. Burke, author of a Chapter about sex within *The Sjögren's Book* edited by DJ Wallace (Sjögren's Foundation and OUP, 2022). Known symptoms of vaginal dryness, pelvic pain, fatigue, low libido or desire arousal not only have an impact and interfere with sexual health. The experts warn also about the gynaecological and urologic complications due to chronic vulvo-vaginal atrophy, including increased risks of sexually transmitted infections, malignancies, endometriosis, lichen sclerosus, ovarian failure, amyloidosis and difficult pregnancies with fetuses subject to increased risk of heart block (neonatal lupus).

(3) Medical attention to   problems around sexuality remain still confined within the psychiatric and psychological domains, ignored by endocrinology, immunology or molecular medicine even when there are hallmarks of autoimmune diseases or even inborn errors of immunity behind sexual dysfunctions. Women are more penalised by this state of affairs within medicine: medicine has traditionally studied male sexual dysfunctions, mostly identified with erectile problems and premature ejaculation, whereas   the interest   to study and treat female sexual dysfunction from a biologic perspective remains still limited, associated with neurological disease (such as stroke, spinal cord injures, Parkinsonism, peripheral neuropathies), with trauma,

sexual abuse, genital surgery, diabetes, liver or renal failure, side effects of medications, and cardiovascular disease.

The 2017 edition of *Harrison's Endocrinology* warns about an evident gender bias, because "although there are anatomical differences as well as variation in the density of vascular and neural beds in males and females, the primary effectors of sexual response are strikingly similar" (see Chapter 19 in: Jameson, J L (editor), *Harrison's Endocrinology*, 4th ed, Mc-Graw Hill, 2017, p. 249).

(4) Today juvenile Sjögren's is still a difficult disease to diagnose without biomarkers. Some specialists require also painful and risky, and very much often inconclusive, biopsies of glands to make a diagnosis, but it seems consensus has been reached at least in that: distinctive signs of paediatric manifestations of the disease consist of parotitis and enlarged lymph nodes. They should be relatively easy hallmarks to recognise. The Sjögren's Foundation has informative materials about Sjögren's in Children. Clinical recommendations exist for the condition also in the UK. See: Price, E. et al., *British Society for Rheumatology guideline on management of adult and juvenile onset Sjögren disease*, Rheumatology, 2024, Rheumatology, 2024, 00, 1–3.

Sinéad And The Sound Of My Heart

Sinéad sent email and text messages I quickly scanned to get the gist. I discarded them straightaway, at first. I did not know her. I had a feeling she was a troll, or something like that (*"sorry for bothering you, I have found you live in London and I followed your posts to the forum of the Sjögren's UK Association. I think I have medical documents that belong to you, dated 1973 and 1975, found in my grandfather correspondence. I understand these are related to your heart murmur, they can be very important since you are researching your autoimmune disease. Please contact me....*").

Oh dear. I did not live in this Country in the 1970s. This must be one of the recent invasive AI designed scams. I threw the messages in the bin. Then she phoned me up. A professional pest, I thought.

I was about to insult her for harassing me and hang up when something froze my brain: she spoke quickly, with an anxious voice, whispering. I couldn't avoid listening. She repeated what she had already written in the messages, but for dropping names and details: she discovered something in her mother's attic, a letter her maternal grandfather Giulio Tomei must have written but not posted to my mother, with attached a medical certificate, blood test results and my full name and date of birth on it, handwritten in capital letters in the top right margin, plus other documents with other logos of Italian hospitals.

I swallowed the question I had on my tongue (Why are you harassing me? What do you want?) because I remembered vividly that name. *Dottor* Tomei rang a bell. My mother was used to see him frequently before her legal separation. Giulio Tomei was her gynaecologist but also a friend of hers in the years of her "liberation and emancipation".

This is how I got hooked into Sinéad's urgency to meet me.

She wanted to give me the documents. I would have actually avoided it. Curiosity prevailed. We arranged this appointment.

We meet in a pub close to Sinéad's office. I arrive early. Just a couple of elderly tourists are silently staring at the menu in a corner. A girl at the counter is busy with crockery. The fan from the ceiling is whooshing slowly. England is not used to heatwaves, not even in the summer. The noise reminds me why I am here: there may be something I need to know about the heart murmur of my childhood. The "whooshing or swishing noise" of the heart in the breathing pattern is what can be heard by doctors using a stethoscope: an extra unusual sound in the heartbeat is considered typical of heart murmuring (1).

I still have strange, brief moments of arrhythmia occasionally. They come and go with tightness of chest, or palpitations, lasting one hour or less, especially under stress. I just got used to it. There have been long periods in my life in which I had up to 90 beats per minute and others with only 64 or 65. One learns to adapt. But the diagnosis of heart murmur haunted me for several years around the age of menarche and did cause enormous distress. After the menopause, I discovered having arrhythmia is also common in any thyroid disorder, so to say... When I was a teenager anaemia was a spectre always present in every conversation my mother had about my health with teachers or other parents. It was an excuse, I believed, to keep me locked in the house (*"Eh, sapesse... mia figlia ha il soffio al cuore"*). Her attitude to deny I could, should, needed to have a social life seemed cruel and hysterical, always masqueraded by an ostentation of maternal care: I should not risk this or that, because of my heart murmur.

Following some other classmates, I joined the Scouts. I was so happy to be a Scout guide. I could have enjoyed many more excursions but also those had to be terminated. I was allowed to visit classmates' houses or the library but only if that was compatible with my brothers' schedules: I had to pick up the younger from nursery and then from his primary school, while she would collect the older from a special primary school. Then I had to do a number of tasks in the kitchen. Every time I wanted to see my friends or do something that was totally obvious for any of my classmates, my mother would say that I couldn't. Why? Because I had anaemia, and the heart murmur.

The diagnosis of heart murmur, together with the hypothesis I had mediterranean anaemia, was accepted by the head of my secondary school without objections: I should not take part in any physical education class, because of my condition.

For a couple of years I was monitored with electrocardiograms every three or four months, confirming my heart was making that strange sound, for mother's sake.

However, at some point, the problem... swooshed away from me and my troubled, borderline mum. Nobody mentioned it anymore. In the meantime I had developed other health issues, so there was no celebration. A physiotherapy program sorted out an abnormal curve in my spine (it was scoliosis). But I had already lost any confidence in the ability of my body to perform whatever sport.

When I started work the music changed. I went to live on my own. I decided to join a gym in the evening. I felt it was the right thing to do. It was around my 20th birthday. The 1980s were promoting the idea of fitness, body building: healthy yuppies' bodies were everywhere. Physical exercise was a revelation: it is never to late for the body to start exercising. For me, it was like a rebirth.

"Are you ok?" asks the waitress leaning forward.

"I am, thank you. I am waiting for a friend. Can I have a green tea please".

Sinéad keeps talking softly, I can barely hear what she is saying while I am trying to connect all the dots she is referring to. It is like she is carrying forward a grievance that has passed from mother to daughter through generations for some reason. There is something familiar to me in the way she talks about her parents and grandparents, something evoking those unexpected turns and twists of life, disease, and endurance always glued with parental love, or the absence of it. She must have been very attached to her mum, and her grandad too.

Antonia, Sinéad's mum, relocated to London with her retired but still very active dad, Giulio Tomei, after he closed his practice in Calabria in the late 1980s. Antonia married in the mid 1990s with Kevin. She worked for the House of Lords but I do not get what exactly Sinéad's mother profession was. Once widowed, and deeply attached to his only daughter, Antonia's father Giulio found he had enough of being a progressivist medic in the South of Italy. After almost four decades of front line work he opted to come and live here in London with Antonia and his son-in-law.

He had kept connections with English professional acquaintances and medical circles for the entirety of his career: he spoke English fluently and always wanted Antonia to study and work in London, far away from the insults of the anti-abortionists, and the death threats he had to cope with for the entirety of his career.

Sinéad pauses to ask if I ever met him, Giulio. Well, yes, I say, but truth is that I do have to delve into the deep end of my childhood to find a vague visual memory of the gynaecologist. I know I was eight or nine years old. He liked sportive cars and was enthusiast about them, he wanted everybody to admire his cars not for vanity, but because he really liked to showcase his passion, and share it with everyone. I am afraid I do not remember much. My mother was one of the many patients he managed to befriend. He was very sociable. But as far as I can remember the relationship with my mum was mostly at a distance, and never involving romance or sex: they exchanged postcards, letters, telephone calls, gossips, political views, those sort of celebrations of male-female friendship during the "liberation and emancipation" movement. And we lived in different towns, so there were few occasions for them to see each other while going out for shopping. Meetings in person were occasional and in connection with medical appointments. He was her gynaecologist, first of all.

Sinéad says she can imagine how was he like as a friend, because she still misses his energy, that lasted til the very end of his life: he enjoyed meeting and arguing with old colleagues in this very pub where we are now, in Bloomsbury, and forget he had promised to come for dinner!

Looking at the attaché case she put on the table, Sinéad says that when he moved to London Giulio brought here also its entire archive, medical notes, records of patients, books, papers, some peculiar pieces of furniture from his studio. She asks me if people in Italy tend to do this. I was expecting her to come to the reason of this appointment. So the question sounds as a digression that irritates me: does she think I am here to be interviewed for an anthropology dissertation?

"I have no idea." I say, annoyed.

I feel she has sensed my irritation, and my desire to cut this encounter shortly, as she's blushing. In turn, I immediately feel guilty, and embarrassed for her, at the same time. I have been her age, asking older people, colleagues, professors, friends of friends, to talk to me about their world, in the hope of making sense of mine.

"How did he die?" I hear myself asking smoothly, with an amiable tone. I regret that I've sorted out to prompt her to continue talking, instead of stopping her chatting and go to the point. But that's the power of heritage, or ancestry, I suppose. We are bonded by invisible strings.

He died of cancer in 2008, at the age of 84. And the same happened unexpectedly to Antonia in 2013, leaving Kevin and Sinéad totally bushed.

Jesus Christ, why did I come to meet this young woman, I think, hurt. I should be minding my own pilates sessions instead.

Sinéad looks either in distress or in the process of acting a drama I do not understand the rationale of. Above all, I do not want to have anything to do with her grievance.

After further particulars about her late mother and the impact of cancer on the whole family life, she eventually arrives to the present day: her dad decided to return to Northern Ireland where he will retire, as he still owns, and manage, a family estate there. He will live with his brother and their elderly mother. Sinéad agreed to sell the big detached house where she grew up, in Sydenham, South London, and buy a flat around here where she works as a market research and account executive for a large advertising group. Her future is here in central London.

That is why she got involved in cleaning the attic, and dismantling all Giulio's cabinets and files. A shredding company has been contracted in preparation for living the family house: they should come to collect all the documentation by the end of the month, according to Kevin's instructions. Sinéad wanted more time, to go through all those boxes, drawers and folders, checking that there wasn't anything personal belonging to Antonia or Giulio they were inadvertently throwing away. She has been discovering so many things about her mother and grandfather she had no clue about after they died. She explains that having studied archeology and being involved in a local group of people passionate about it, she finds the reconstruction of past events irresistible: past fragments keep haunting her, begging for stories.

The letter is attached to the rest of the documents with a golden clip, one of those used for banknotes years ago. Interesting, but she took it away handing over the sheet of paper to me: perhaps she does have some sense of what is property, and boundaries, and privacy, and authenticity. She thinks the letter belongs to my mum, but the golden clip is hers.

The calligraphy on the letter is very legible and that is unusual for a doctor. I was expecting to have problems reading it, I say. Instead I read it aloud very easily, it is in Italian. Sinéad says she doesn't speak the language but she can understand it:

Cara A.

Grazie per l'olio di frantoio, che pensiero stupendo e graditissimo. Ma mi dispiace che ti sei disturbata. Tu non devi ringraziarmi per nulla. Sei come una sorella. Dovere mio aiutarti in queste disgraziate circostanze. Guarda avanti. Tutto a posto per B. Amici fidatissimi all'Università hanno visto i risultati degli esami e mi hanno assicurato che il direttore della casa farmaceutica la metterà in lista, B. ha esattamente il profilo ematologico che volevano. Qualsiasi cosa succeda a te e a tuo marito sarà sempre assistita e in buone mani ovunque vi troviate. Ti auguro una pronta ripresa. Quando scendi da queste parti chiama e ti porto a Reggio con la Ferrari per una granita di caffè con panna. Con affetto. Tuo Giulio

Among the documents, Sinéad wants me to have a look at another one in particular.

"This is what I mentioned in my messages" she whispers solemnly, with excitement.

I am just slightly shocked to see all these references to real people and places that remind me at once of another world, another Century.

There is a memo, typewritten on the letterhead of one of the Universities of Rome, addressed to Dr. Giulio Tomei, in which I immediately see there is my name as well, it is in the "Re:", the subject.

"I don't remember I have ever been in any hospital in Rome as a child" I say, instinctively. "Nor that any doctor or professor from that University ever visited me".

Sinéad does not seem concerned at all. Instead she asks me (although it sounds like she is suggesting) if Tomei could have obtained these documents from my mother. If so, he could have taken my medical records because he wanted to give them to those people in Rome.

"Well, yes, it is not completely implausible" I concede to her fantasy. But I think I would really like to go home and not waste my time with this girl. Yet I am really feeling entrapped and intrigued by Sinéad's investigations into my childhood, and alleged medical history.

My memory spins quickly: very likely there were several occasions in which I needed blood tests around that age. And mum remained in contact with Tomei for few years in the early 1970s. However, I can hardly believe that all this paperwork has gone back and forth between North, South and Central Italy and then ended up following the retired gynaecologist in an attic in central London, to be kept with a tidy handwritten letter he wrote but did not post to my mum.

Above all, who cares? Why the hell am I here, into a phishing set?

I would like to ask her how did she ended up working in advertising, but I do not dare, as I want to go home as soon as possible. She continues with a slow moving torrent of intimate details about the life of somebody so weakly connected to me. And yet I am intrigued, I wonder why Giulio's later life was here in London, if my mother knew, if there was any relevance for our family as well, and my mind fires back flashing memories of me and my mum in Giulio's racing cars on the narrow, terrifying road in the very south wild west coast of Calabria (before they built a motorway, with very high bridges). It was, and perhaps it still is, the Mediterranean version of Highway 1 in California.

However, nothing from these memories brings back anything important to me, and I am afraid the fact that I might have suffered from anaemia as a child would not be, per se, considered by any rheumatologist as a sign of juvenile Sjögren's onset neither (2). I try to put this consideration to her attention as I continue to feel suspicious, like I had been targeted with a scam by this possibly very astute young advertising pro.

Why on earth somebody should be googling my name and date of birth, and keep medical documents produced fifty years ago instead of shredding them straightaway? I am confused, I say to her candidly.

The idea that Giulio Tomei brought to London, in his retirement, all the confidential information about his patients - and the children of his patients. - really does not match the vague memory I have of a handsome wealthy man, with his luxurious cars, and some frames with glamorous pictures of American skylines in the waiting room of his Calabrian medical studio. Instead, I could imagine he came to London to join clubs for vintage cars owners, for instance, or to make friends with other owners of Lamborghini, Porsche, Ferrari cars, etcetera. Yet, like brain fog has locked me in, I cannot resist to ask her: "Do you know why he had pictures of American cities and skyscrapers in his medical studio? It was something very unusual for a doctor, I remember I found them quite strange.".

"Oh, I did not know that" she blushes again. I regret I asked.

She suggests they could be souvenirs of his American years.

"American years?" I am utterly bewildered, totally on the hook.

"Yes, in his youth, I think it was in the late 1940s, he travelled all over the world", she keeps saying. "He spent over two years in the United States, recruiting and then assisting pregnant women for a famous program at the Vanderbilt University Hospital Prenatal Clinic. He was there as a PhD student, I found his proposal for a study, but then he joined the research programme for another study supported by the USA Public Health Service and the Rockefeller Foundation on the effect of radioactive iron, that was infamously known as the "vitamin cocktail" nutrition program (3). I read about this also in one of his monumental photographic albums I just browsed last night".

Sinéad is ecstatic. She really wants to tell me about her discoveries in the attic.

"Wow" I am genuinely impressed, and moved. "Who would have thought that my mother's gynaecologist from Calabria had such an international career."

"And a blue blood family of means, to send him all over the world" she continues, proud of her grandfather's family. "It was because he was really passionate about his patients and did not really need a salary that he kept all those records, including yours. He wanted to make a lasting service."

Nothing comes out from this conversation.

I try to reassure Sinéad that there is anything really important to me in these old documents, the authenticity of which I honestly doubt. I recommend to go ahead with the shredding company without further ado. I see now clearly that the perseverance of her imagination and her strong interest in her own family history wanted to create a story out of very much nothing consistent with my reminiscences.

I wonder if at the beginning of my career I had this sort of imaginative investigative, constructive attitude. I do not think so.

I would like to get out of the pub as soon as possible but I see she looks at me with an expression of genuine regret for the waste of time, for the allegations, for the invasion of privacy, for everything.

"I am so sorry, I thought it was something very important you wanted to reconnect with" she says. Suddenly she is not smiling anymore, she looks very frustrated. I feel I have to explain to her the rationale of my palpable irritation and discomfort.

Anaemia mediterranean, as far as I can say, is an expression that in the early 1970s was still used indiscriminately in all cases of common anaemia and thalassemia (the most serious form of anaemia). This is indeed a serious genetic disorder but I am sure I did not have this disease as a child. I had lot of issues, probably above average, around the age of my menarche, and for some time there must have been also medics' worries about my health. My mum was terrified that I could have a diagnosis of thalassaemia or any other incurable disease. She was used to talk with everybody frantically about health issues. She would say, generally speaking, that I was anaemic, and that I had the heart murmur, something I can remember with a degree of certainty because it did affect my social life for years. At her funeral, a former colleague of hers kindly came to speak with meand she wanted to know how I was coping with my Mediterranean anaemia!

"Oh, dear" Sinéad sit back on her chair and eventually smiles again. "I see. So your mum died?

"Yes, few years ago" I say, breathing out deeply. For some reason she must have thought my mum was still alive. "It's alright" I add.

"She had a life lived to the full of her possibilities. So what I reckon is that at some point, maybe before or after one of their exciting rides with your grandad in a Ferrari along the Calabrian sea coast, she must have said to your grandfather that she was very worried about me. For a certain period of time, while she was separating from my father, she had quite severe mental health crises. She was prescribed strong medications, she had a very complex relationship with my grandmother, who agreed with my dad in declaring my mum culpable for ruining the family in the attempt of halting the separation proceedings. Divorce was a huge thing in Southern Italy in the early 1970s, and my mum was terrified that she could not care for the three of us... At a certain point she started saying quite obsessively she would run away, take her own life, abandon us all, causing me to panic. She was very confused, but I felt I had to appease her in any possible way. Perhaps my heart murmur was because of that fear we both have not to be able to live far away from my dad. But as far as the anaemia thing is concerned, you know, there were no genetic tests at the time, so very likely the disease was something hypothesised, suspected, but not actually diagnosed. In any case, I can assure you that if I suffered from it, it must have been a very mild or temporary disease mimicking the condition, without long term consequences on my health. I do not believe it has had any part in the development of my autoimmunity, for instance. For some years my mum also mentioned very frequently I had rheumatism as a child, while talking about my health, and that was even a stickier label compared to that of heart murmur. I remember my grandmother was always saying to me I shouldn't touch the cold water because I had rheumatisms. Even swimming in the sea was something that could bring risks to my health. But I really do not know how they were used to give those diagnoses of genetic-something back in the day. My research has limited historical remit, you know..."

I have tried to steer again the conversation in the direction of a more lighthearted chat, and to make sure she does not want to insist saying she has discovered, and is now holding important medical documents that belong to me, I gave her another story to think about, based on my own memories. I smile while I finish my tea.

She seems to agree she needs to look things in a different ways but for continuing with her free associations: "It looks like your mother found her own way to exclude you could have anaemia, in a certain sense, cathartically, talking about it at all times with everybody..."

"Well, I guess one could say so in a novel..." I conclude.

She insists: "What I do not understand is why Giulio kept the correspondence with your mum, and kept also your electrocardiograms here together with the medical records" she clearly wants me to validate somehow she made some important discoveries, and convince me I have to go trough the documents, one by one, in any case.

"Yes" I make a further effort to hint at a rationale, patiently, disclosing further memories of mine: "When I started my secondary school mum found a cardiologist who looked into all my blood tests, visited me very thoroughly, made several electrocardiograms and gave us reassurance and instructions on what should be done in order to get peace of mind on that scary menace of an haemolytic condition: monitoring, exams, that sort of things.   After about one year we forgot the whole issue of suspected thalassaemia, and the heart murmur altogether. Life went on galloping". I hope I made it clear.

"My symptoms of extreme weakness disappeared" I add "perhaps thanks to better nutrients and vitamins, but not the fatigue and the anxiety that have been coming back in many other occasions, in connection with other symptoms later on. That is what motivated me to research autoimmune diseases, as you have seen from my online posts".

I see she remains unconvinced, or just disappointed. She makes a third or fourth attempt to pass me the letter and I say probably raising my voice "You can keep it, shred it together with the whole file".

Then I feel a sense of calm, or mindfulness. I lend back on my feet from somewhere, and I want to dissipate all the narrative Sinéad has been evidently mounting from these documents, whatever they are, genuine or fake, and however they have been found, or fabricated.

I ask Sinéad, and I try not to sound too much aggressive or rude now, but I hear my tone of voice has changed as I am not trying anymore to appear neither blasé nor irritated, why she "just" wanted me to have these materials.

She does not have an answer to this. On the contrary, she is very much surprised I wondered the question.

"These are your medical records, this is your own health." she says, like she is mentioning the Bible, or God, or something else of overarching importance.

"Not at all, you are confusing different levels of reality, there is much more of myself and my health in the traces I left on this tea mug than on the entire package of documents fifty years old collated by your grandfather."

I reiterate that the entire medical evidence she thinks she has found seems to me actually a whipped up narrative to build up a reality on social media, connecting bits and pieces of people lives across time and geography, or preparing a scam.

She objects, almost passionately, that the data "must be" very relevant to my work on the causes of Sjögren's today.

What a nutter, this girl has built in her head an entire script about my research on autoimmune diseases and she thinks I have to align to it.

I see that she may be genuinely fascinated with the idea that serendipity brings all of us together, and scientific discoveries spark out magically from feelings of togetherness because we are all interconnected etcetera etcetera.

I am an old dog. I do not have any desire to know more about these narratives, about her, about her intrusions in my past or in anybody's else past. I just say to her: "Science does not work this way. Science communication neither. You cannot really think you do storytelling manipulating real people records, can you?"

I do not want to explain to her how complex is any investigation into the aetiology of autoimmune diseases.

"Well", I concede trying to smile about the whole thing: "It is true that understanding autoimmunity requires a certain degree of imagination, bringing together all sorts of data: scientists all over the world are trying to do so. However no, Sinéad, I do not need and I do not want any... how can I say, scavenging? of medical notes and records, personal recollections of medical problems and so on, the reliability of which, you understand, is highly questionable. In order to substantiate any narrative, any story, you have to achieve a degree of certainty that goes well beyond traces or even serious evidence that would be alright for a fictional project, do you understand?"

"But these are your data" she insists. She seems disappointed that I am off the hook now.

"I do have to go" I say, grabbing nervously my phone and the credit card to pay the pub. "Please go ahead and shred all these documents Sinéad, I do appreciate all your concerns and interest. And I will keep you posted about my book if you wish".

She understands it is over.

We shake hands cordially and eventually I am out of the pub. I feel I am almost running down the road while I am walking towards the underground. A myriad of flashing memories from those years returns to swish again back and forth in my mind, seeking anchorage points to the present. And there aren't any.

I spent an afternoon tried to explain to a young stranger how to deal with matters she does not know or does not understand but may have an impact on rights to privacy of living people.

I gave her lot of additional personal information, hopefully to make her able to direct her curiosity in a direction that makes sense for the present.

I usually have raised inflammation and a lower than average count of white blood cells - perhaps this is the main thing that, with ups and downs, has remained constant for my entire life, since the times of the controversial diagnosis of heart murmur. Together with other signs of inflammation or potential allergies, this biomarker is quite common in the blood tests of people with any autoimmune disease.

As far as the heart murmur is concerned, I explained that most heart murmurs that were seen as possible signs of serious diseases in my childhood are now considered harmless, associated with adjustments the body make while growing up during the adolescence, and not necessarily a sign of any juvenile onset of Sjögren's or other autoimmune disease. Also anaemia resolves very often after puberty, especially with the right diet and lifestyle. However it is true that if it persists is considered among the predictors of non-Hodgkin lymphoma (2). All in all, if there is any lesson to learn from scavenging old medical records and personal data, is that everything changes in life: without a context, biomarkers as well as letters to friends have no meaning. I do not know if I have succeeded in giving her some contextual elements but I do hope Sinéad will mind her own business from now on. Thank goddess, the train is here.

At home, I cannot avoid to go back to my own research files looking for something I'd like to review. I remember I have read somewhere that anaemia in Sjögren's may develop because the bone marrow is exhausted, because of too recurrent bursts of inflammation in the body. At a young age, it might be just a very common iron deficiency associated anaemia, especially for girls that have a very early menarche, that triggers spirals of inflammation in the body.

Truth is that everybody in my family experienced great stress in the years Sinéad has brought back to my memory. Mum might have asked for help to Tomei in one her tantrums for not being able to sort out things as she would have liked to. And what I am doing now? I smile to myself because, like my mother, I am prone to ruminations.

My mum's trust in medicine was much higher than mine: she was convinced that doctors' could and should solve any problem. It never crossed her mind that my heart was just murmuring I needed love, peace, and rest, more than medicine.

Nobody has ever tested me for inborn errors of immunity or any other genetic predisposition to haemolytic diseases. Over the years my blood tests have showed all sorts of slightly weird characteristics, sometimes mild, sometimes more alarming. This is not uncommon for people diagnosed with Sjögren's, a prototypical autoimmune disease that can lead, among other haematologic abnormalities, to hypo-complementemia (2).

Abnormalities in the haematologic profile of people with Sjögren's show in a crazy variety of patterns of alterations compared to "normal" serological values. Such great heterogeneity of non specific signs, often dismissed as minor issues, nonetheless clearly indicates that something in the blood is not quite right, but is really hard for doctors to make sense of it in a consistent framework of interpretations, due to the possible concurrent presence of many other non specific symptoms. So that it is true, as probably Sinéad's intuition wanted to point out, that some early signs, seen in retrospect, acquire more significance. Anaemia is recurrent among those Sjögren's patient who suffer from severe cytopenia at some point in life, for instance. Therefore the best way to assess risks of autoimmunity in relation to these conditions is, or should be, to count haemoglobin, as my mum did for some time in my teens and after, perhaps without exactly knowing why.

The indignation for what I decided was Sinéad's attempt to trick me in a sort of social media scam is fading away. I inhale and exhale, feeling the ease of my breathing tonight, and everything is alright, in spite of the agitation the alleged "discovery" in the paperwork of *Dottor* Tomei has caused me.

It was a bizarre encounter. Something interesting, all in all. I think to my supper, ready, waiting for me in my small kitchenette. I smile to myself, to the self, to the non-self and ...whatever self I am made of. Sinéad succeeded in the almost impossible mission of dating me, with the allure of unknown personal data allegedly from my childhood.

It does not really matter if Tomei's letter to my mum was a well fabricated fake or a genuine document. In any case it would have been unconceivable for her at that time to entrust my care to a friend, or to friends of friends. It's a relief to think that yes, she was quite frantic, and at times abusive in her obsessive ways to control my life, but she did enrol me in a lifelong habit of looking after my blood test results, and listening to the sound of my heart while seeking more and more knowledge.

The day after I wake up in a heavy sweat.
I dreamt of my father bargaining my jewels in a little poach, and also myself, with some poker players at Stazione Termini in Rome. In this nightmare, Sinéad turned up as a journalist who was investigating cases of Münchausen syndrome by proxy, another way to talk about medical child abuse in which parents, or other caregivers, falsify medical records of children creating illnesses, or the appearance of illnesses, that do not actually exist, giving exaggerated or distorted accounts of medical history, altering labs reports or inducing genuine illnesses.
What a fantasy, what a phishing architect that Sinéad. (4)

Notes

(1) The British Heart Foundation explains on their website that such "extra noise happens when your blood doesn't flow smoothly through your heart".
(2) Low complement values in the blood are considered a sign of an increased risk of lymphoma, or propensity to develop blood cancers according to the current clinical guideline. See: Price E J et al, *British Society for Rheumatology guideline on management of adult and juvenile onset Sjögren disease*, Rheumatology, 2024, 00, 1–31. On the peculiarities of the disease and its clinical guideline see also: Both, T et al, *Reviewing primary Sjögren's syndrome: beyond the dryness - From pathophysiology to diagnosis and treatment*, Int. J. Med. Sci. 2017, Vol. 14; Ramos-Casals M et al, *Primary Sjogren syndrome: hematologic patterns of disease expression,* Medicine. 2002; 81: 281-92.
(3) Frankenburg, F.R. (editor), *Human medical experimentation: from smallpox vaccines to secret government programs*, Greenwood, 2917, p. 239-241 notes that: "In 1993, following revelations about the large

number of radiation experiments carried out in the United States during the Cold War period, reports about the Vanderbilt experiments appeared in the Nashville press. Litigators contacted some of the women involved in the original study. At the class-action trial that followed, experts called by both sides disagreed about the amount of radioactivity to which the women and their children had been exposed and whether there was a significant increase in cancer in the fetuses exposed to the radioiron. Vanderbilt attorneys argued that the researchers were behaving like all researchers at the time and should not be judged by standards of 40 years later. The case was settled out of court. Vanderbilt agreed to pay the women $10 million and to apologise. (…) The Vanderbilt studies increased our understanding of iron absorption. While it is impossible to determine whether they caused any harm to the subjects, it is certain that they offered no benefit to the schoolchildren, pregnant women, or their fetuses. The studies were not a secret in the medical community or even in the community at large, but the children, their parents, their school board, and the pregnant women involved were never informed that they were being exposed to radioactivity, nor of the possible risks they might have incurred through exposure."

(4) Mitchell, SA, Creamer, L, Spencer MJ, *Medical child abuse / Munchausen Syndrome by proxy*, in Child Abuse: Quick Reference, 3rd edition, STM Learning, 2017.

The Surgeon With The Parakeets
And The Lost Appendix

He called 101 four times over the last eighteen months. He even tried to talk with 999 in one occasion. This time the police officer cut the interview short to say they would come soon.

"How soon?"

"By noon this morning, do not touch anything".

"There will be an inspection" he announced, triumphant, to his wife.

"The Police is coming here, darling?" Josephine's stubborn Scottish accent usually fended off when she was alarmed.

They did not have a proper breakfast this morning, she insisted. Back and forth from the garden, the shed, the phone.

"Did you go to the garden last night? Did you lock the shed door last night?" He asked for at least half an hour, back and forth, in despair.

"Oh dear, was that really necessary? Finish your tea, please. What can they do this time around coming here? For an inspection?"

She was used to repeat word by word what he had just said. She started doing it as a tactic, trying to make him more reasonable, and at first it worked. But his mental health had so deteriorated over the last couple of years that sometimes he now seemed lost in a wood: alone in his mind, she could not reach him anymore. He could deny what he said, or forget it, and change his mind at the last minute jeopardising plans, upsetting friends. Other times, he still seemed reasonable and in control. He could calm down after a crisis, talk about something else, totally unrelated or inconsequential, do his gym exercises, work in the garden.

"They come to inspect the shed" he explained laconic, finished his tea in one draught and swiftly made his way upstairs to wash and change.

He talked loudly with Josephine, or to himself, from the bedroom: he wanted a certain t-shirt he could not find, and wear certain trousers and not the lounging ones, and would not it better if he took a shower and shaved before their arrival?

She should welcome them and offer tea if they come sooner, he shouted over the banister. He then started ruminating answers to questions he imagined the police may ask. He should introduce himself, a retired academic and surgeon, and perhaps explain why he had such an unusual hobby, because these birds are not frequently seen as pets, and not even frequently seen at all in London.

The first thing to know about Professor Fedele Labutta was that hadn't he become a famous gastroenterologist surgeon, and Emeritus Professor, he would have chosen a career as zoologist, and studied some species of ring-necked parakeets - namely the Alexandrine (Psittacula eupatria), the Blue-crowned (Aratinga acuticaudata) and the Monk (Myopsitta monachus) parakeets.

The Alexandrine Parakeet was the one with a purplish shoulder, his favourite. Bright green, with   long tails, these birds were now very entertaining in the dashing summer light in parks and gardens in South London. When he and Josephine started breeding them, years ago, they were still rare, weird birds to see in British skies and greens.

Breeding parakeets was a passion, accidentally sparked when he was 14 years old and went to Giardini Zoologici in Rome with his mother, a former Russian ballerina of Jewish descent, like his father. And yes, today he shares the love for the Alexandrine with Josephine.

His academic career was a priority and for several years he did not think about the parrots. He published pioneering papers about laparoscopy, introduced new procedures for less invasive surgery, especially for stomach cancers.

They tried to have children, in vain. Josephine was a proud lab technician (now she would be called bioinformatician), keen on following his husband everywhere: they had been together since their secondary school, a story of true friendship and then happy marriage. They had no time to regret being childless. They have been distracted by so many interests, including travelling. Then the parrots came along, and indeed caring for the birds requires lot of time.

The opportunity to move to London arrived in the 1980s when Josephine found irresistible the idea he could work for University College Hospital. This was after his mother died, and they did not have any particular reason to remain in Rome anymore while Josephine had siblings living in Scotland and Wales she would have liked to visit more often. He was 52-years-old, she 51, and did not take long for Josephine to convince him: this could be his last very important move in a remarkable career. She could work as a secondary school teacher, or in a lab, if she really wanted to.

So they began a new life in England in their 50s. It was fun, Josephine would say chatting with their many younger academic friends and new neighbours years later, when a new Italian diaspora, the so called "brain drain" in the 2000s, brought to London many young Italian researchers, writers, weirdos from all walks of cultural and scientific life.

However, from time to time, somebody would insistently ask why they left Rome for London, back in the day. Fedele would then talk about his family: Giovanni, his father, whose academic career in mathematics was affected by the fascist racial laws, left the Country for America, to never return, in the 1930s. His mother Dorotha took Fedele and his brother Aldo to Milan, in incognito: she managed to find a safe job as entertainer in a night club with a rich clientele. Being very close to a wealthy director of La Scala Theatre in Milan, Dorotha made sure he and his brother grew up without missing anything. For several years, until he moved back to Rome to go to the University there, they lived in a big house along the Navigli, where Aldo unexpectedly died at the very young age of 18 of a rare brain tumour. That triggered Fedele's interest for medicine. They were introduced to famous Professors, international specialists, consultants very well connected with eclectic artists like his mother. It was in that distinctive Milan intellighenzia, with lot of international contacts, that he was lucky enough to meet his future wife, from a wealthy protestant diplomatic family.

People would become slightly confused to hear Labutta talking about all those family stories of emigration, death, destiny, ups and downs. But this was pretty much what he would always says to everybody, in lively small talks: for more than thirty years now, he always introduced himself and his family like they had a script for social occasions. Everybody would find their story so interesting. However, Josephine would try to drop the subject at some point, saying they were now happy in a lovely detached house not far away from Kew, with a big shed for the parakeets in the back garden.

That juvenile Fedele's passion for birds reignited to become a singular hobby for an elderly couple: breeding parrots in West London. When they arrived here they had just a small cage with four

Alexandrine. Over time these multiplied. They now also have the Blue-crowned, plus the Monk ones. In case the police asked, Josephine knows how to show the differences.

The doorbell buzzed loudly.
"Jo, the door. they have arrived.", he shouts while still rehearsing his introduction, after he shaved.
Assistant Chief Constable Daniel Lowe stood on the doormat. His taller colleague Police Constable (PC) Thomas Hardy looked down at Fedele from behind Lowe's shoulder.
"Professor Labutta I suppose?", Assistant Chief Constable Lowe introduced himself and his colleague PC Hardy, and went straight to the point: "We are here to take your statement and inspect the shed, Professor".
"Thank you, thank you. Please come through", he was ceremonious. That sounded a bit odd.
"Can I bring you some tea or coffee?" Josephine asked, in need of sending a signal to the police officers: to slow down, please, before his husband could get confused, while they took a seat at the long oak table.
"A cup of tea would be nice".
Perhaps Assistant Chief Constable Lowe understood, somehow, that Professor Labutta suffers from age related dementia or perhaps Alzheimer's: the disease, is featured on the cover of a magazine on the table, by the way.
Josephine went towards a corner in the kitchen, opposite to the big living room. They had wanted this house exactly because they liked the open space on the floor, with a beautiful view of the garden through large glass doors.
The Assistant Chief Constable spoke clearly and loudly: "We are here to help. Since you have already made three times an accusation towards… what's the name of the guy, Thomas?" He asks PC Hardy.
"Jon Thorn" the tall man replied promptly.
"Mr Thorn, right. You have accused him to steal your birds in other two occasions Professor. But we haven't found absolutely any evidence to corroborate this accusation. We talked with Mr Thorn, visited him at home last time you reported him, found he did not have any bird, and he also expressed his deep sympathy, and concern, that

you might have mistaken him for someone else, perhaps somebody living in the neighbourhood, closer to you…"

Assistant Chief Constable Lowe looked at his colleague's notes, to make sure PC Hardy was writing down something.

"He's not my neighbour" Labutta raised his voice.

"Well, he lives down the road" Daniel Lowe contradicted him with a pinch of confrontational tone, that he regretted straightaway. In fact, Labutta raised his voice even more.

"Yes, but he's not my neighbour" he almost shouted.

"Alright Professor Labutta. No problem" Assistant Chief Constable Lowe looked around, to see if the wife was coming along to help. He silently swore and wondered why Chief Superintendent always send him for these "delicate" jobs in the community. There were other colleagues in the Safer Neighbourhood Team who could possibly have more patience and knowledge of what to do with elderly people.

Josephine was still moving crockery around the kettle. Lowe continued with the recollection of evidence they had on file, talking slowly: "Now, Professor Labutta we need to move forward, we have to come to a close on this case, do you understand? It has been going on for some time. We need evidence. Mr Thorn was interviewed on caution after your call last year, he came at the Police Station to make a statement. The duty solicitor was assisting. He declared he knew you since long, because he was a patient of yours, sort of, at some time but he did not even know you had birds in your shed. He declared he never came to your house and met you only a couple of times since he has moved into this ward. We understand the situation is different this time around, as you have suffered a trespass, the shed's padlock was removed from its place, the door open, but nothing is broken or damaged apparently, and some birds were stolen with their cage. So we now have a case of theft on your property and perhaps some criminal damages to be clearly identified, and this makes a difference this time around."

"That's why we are here" PC Hardy added, surprisingly showing a feather of admiration for his superior's synthesis.

"Yes yes" Labutta seemed lost.

The Assistant Chief Constable, reluctantly, asked for the second or third time: "One of your cages is missing and the shed door has been left open, unlocked. Is this correct?"

Labutta was nodding and so Lowe did not wait for an answer. He continued, repeating, trying to get to something: "Well, this means this time we have a trespass case and potentially a criminal offence to deal with. So tell me more about your suspect, have you ever met Jon Thorn?"

"Sure" Fedele Labutta moved a pile of photographic books to the other side of the long table, then he remained silent, staring a void in the direction of his wife. His eyes rolled over the place, and anchored on Josephine who was assembling crockery on a tray. How many times she asked him not to rearrange the cupboards without her.

"Why on earth this guy living down the road should be interested in your birds?" The Assistant Chief Constable insisted, glancing at PC Hardy who, in turn, dropped his pen and looked at Mrs Labutta's, in hope for tea.

"Do you know Mr Thorn is a busy musician working with the Orchestra of the BBC?" Assistant Chief Constable Lowe tried to elicit a sensible answer, something that could resemble a retraction of Labutta's accusation perhaps.

"He is often away, travelling all over the country and also abroad for concerts. At the moment, it seems he is not reachable either, so it is very likely he would say that last night he was working far away from his London home, is that right Thomas?"

"Yes Daniel. We immediately called Mr Thorn's head office this morning after Professor Labutta phoned 101" PC Hardy replied, bang on. "We have been told he is returning home not before next Monday night or Tuesday, so... in a week time".

"In any case we cannot treat him again as a suspect if we do not have some evidence of his involvement" the Assistant Chief Constable concluded.

There was an expression of total dismay on the Professor's face.

Daniel Lowe is a compassionate soul, behind his impatience. He asked Labutta two or three times, leaning on the table, looking at him from above the frame of his glasses: "Professor Labutta? Are you okay?"

After what seemed a very long time, Labutta replied that yes, everything was alright, but he was still looking absent, confused.

Lowe took a sip of tea that Josephine eventually served in the meantime, exchanged a glimpse with her. Then he talked again, slowly: "Please, Professor Labutta, tell me why do you suspect Mr Thorn to have such an interest in your parrots to the point he would come nighttime, trespass crossing your garden from the opening at the back of your fence, break into the shed, allegedly, and steal one cage with your birds".

"And not all of them" PC Hardy added meticulously.

Josephine held his husband's hand on the table.

Assistant Chief Constable Lowe noticed the gesture and took another sip of tea.

The professor exhaled deeply, then said: " I removed his appendix in 1988".

PC Hardy burst into a noisy, cracking laugh for few seconds, embarrassing Lowe who actually almost choked in the effort of restraining himself from doing the same, while he wanted to direct his subordinate to a more appropriate conduct too.

Lowe looked up over his spectacles to see the watery eyes of Mrs Labutta. After breathing in and breathing out in exasperation, in an almost deferential tone he tried to elicit more: "And.... ?"

Josephine whispered: "Darling", touching Labutta's forearm with her other hand.

He was not at all discouraged or perplexed by those reactions. Instead he seemed regaining confidence in his version of the events. He said, quite assertively, he could recollect some facts for the police. He wanted to explain what happened, precisely, and the reason why. Then: "I saw Thorn a couple of years ago at Tesco. He recognised me and reminded me I performed his appendectomy" Labutta spoke firmly, leaving his wife hand on the table to sip his tea. "He recognised me straightaway, but I had absolutely no memory of him. He told me he had just moved into this ward as he married, and left his parents house in Highgate. He told me many particulars, including something very convincing about my operating theatre of those years, so I came to believe he was telling the truth, he must have been a patient of mine indeed. I was used to be at the hospital three days a week plus some emergencies, and I was still teaching full-time. It was a very busy period. I have no idea nor recollection of the many people I operated on. I performed appendectomy probably over a thousand times".

"I see" PC Hardy exhaled, hopeless. He looked at Lowe and stopped taking notes. "Thanks, nice cup of tea" said to Josephine. He thought, like the Assistant Chief Constable, that Labutta must have been completely nuts. But what else could they do in these circumstances?

Labutta continued: "Yes, Thorn told me that his appendectomy happened to be very urgent, with hospital acceptance on a Sunday night and discharge few days later. It really annoyed him a lot as he was just starting his career, but it was one of those things... However he retained a strong memory of that night. He said it happened after he had a big meal at his mother's house and the horrendous abdominal pain convinced her to call an ambulance. Luckily, I said. He agreed on the point that I saved his life, and thanked me for that but he did not seem sincere, he was still in doubt, he admitted, because he had absolutely no previous instance of abdominal or pelvic pain that could suggest he had an inflamed appendix. But that was actually almost turning into peritonitis, I told him".

Suddenly Labutta panted heavily, as he had run up a set of stairs. The pause made Assistant Chief Constable Lowe willing to speak, in the most affable tone he could fake: "Professor Labutta, thank you so much indeed. I think that's all in terms of detailing your relationship with the suspect, or better to say, the accused. You rest assured we put down everything in the report, right Thomas?". PC Hardy nodded.

"Can I see the shed?" Lowe then asks roughly, unexpectedly, looking at Josephine. The elderly lady with watery eyes answered very anxiously that yes, of course they could, her Scottish accent blowing towards the garden.

Then Assistant Chief Constable Lowe tried to release tension, poking at a big frame on the wall: "Madam, is this your portrait?" he asked, while heading towards the glass doors, admiring the perfectly mowed lawn.

The shed was quite big but remained almost hidden in a corner of the back garden with several shrubs slightly, yet purposely, left overgrown on one side, so that the door seemed close at a distance, while it was actually open. There was no sign of force or criminal damage whatsoever.

While they moved around the garden, Labutta kept on talking about the operations he performed on Jon Thorn and on dozens, if not hundreds, of other patients until at least the late 1990s, adding medical particulars on the rationale behind the decision to remove the vermiform little organ. The Professor wanted to explain to the police officers his decision to operate, like the subject of appendectomy was an essential part of the actual investigation about the stolen parakeets. They remained speechless.

Then he returned on the musician: "When I met him at the supermarket, Thorn told me he had read in a flight magazine that surgeons think twice before removing the appendix nowadays. He asked me if I could have saved his appendix, because after the operation he did start suffering from a stubborn Clostridium difficile infection that his GP was unable to treat once and for all, and it wasn't clear how did it happen he got it, where that chronic infection could have come from, out of the blue, after the appendectomy. I tried to reassure him" now Labutta seemed talking as a perfectly sane, confident elderly expert chap giving a lecture to an audience of friendly villains met for tea at the local community center: "I tried to reassure him, I said to him that I myself had my appendectomy removed approximately at the same age, in my 20s, in Milan, but I do not remember I had never had such an issue of clostridium difficile or other infections nor other problems afterwards that could be in connection with the removed appendix. These are very common infections that come and go, you know. It is true that twenty and more years ago we did not have any guideline to follow. The decision for appendectomy was made on the assessment of risks of complications case by case. Perhaps nowadays colleagues have a different protocol before they decide to remove the appendix but, believe me, Thorn's case was a plain, obvious, emergency case, as far as he himself reminded me. It must have been quite an emergency, so we had to operate him straightaway".

"Hm?" Assistant Chief Constable Lowe made an attempt to interrupt the Professor and reiterate the point of the new evidence they needed in order to question Thorn once again, if they decided not to drop the case. In vain, as Labutta was unstoppable now: he continued to give the two police officers a lecture, while the men all stood next to the shed door. Josephine remained halfway, in the middle of the lawn, like waiting for his husband to come back to her.

Until not long ago, Labutta explained, the protocol in case of appendicitis - that is exactly when the appendix become inflamed, perhaps impacted by matters from the intestines or invaded with nasty bacteria - was that the little organ should be surgically removed. Full stop. There was anything to argue about it. Everybody could understand that the appendectomy was needed to prevent further risks to life. But now things are more complicated. There must be an assessment, an investigation in the reasons why the appendix has become inflamed.

Assistant Chief Constable Lowe was moved to smile to himself, perhaps overcoming his frustration: he imagined how other colleagues in other divisions working on serious crimes would simply laugh at a possible referral from his Safer Neighbourhood Team's Chief Superintendent requiring to investigate a case of stolen parakeets in revenge for an appendectomy. This is what they thought local policing was all about: comedy, entertainment, social media, while others do the serious work and protect people from real, not imaginary criminals.

Eventually, Daniel Lowe was able to speak calmly and loudly, with a wit that brought into the conversation his own wife, and gave him an advantage on the surgeon's medical tirade: "My wife also had the appendix removed as a teenager, and she still has a big stretch mark she complains about every summer, because it's visible when she wears a bikini, you know..."

Labutta did not seem to intercept any humour but that call in for another appendix removed slowly made him wrapping up his talk, with sadness. He said he reviewed all the details of the procedure that was in use at the time of Thorn's appendectomy, and there was absolutely nothing wrong with it.

The Assistant Chief Constable pointed his finger at the back of the shed from the threshold: "You have many other birds left here. How many parrots do you have in total Professor Labutta?" He asked.

Josephine came closer to his husband to answer the question, and she took his hand again, moving slowly: "They were 23 and now we have just 17".

"So all the six parrots missing were in one cage, the one stolen?" PC Hardy asked, still waving his pen and notebook.

"Correct, six Alexandrine parakeets" the woman confirmed.

"I see".

Lowe tried to look concerned. He hinted at the need for PC Hardy to keep taking notes but the two men could barely disguise they were smiling at each other now.

Assistant Chief Constable Lowe theatrically signalled to his colleague to come forward and take a picture of the cages at the back of the shed.

After the short lecture about appendectomy, Labutta seemed now very tired and lost in his other world, again.

"So is the appendix that causes irritable bowel syndrome?" Lowe asked, genuinely willing to praise Labutta's expertise, while they all returned inside the house: "My wife also says she has had a frequent upset belly since after her appendectomy".

Labutta seemed returning among them after those moments of void, and with more medical knowledge, but not really answering the question: "the appendix is now considered to play an important role in the development and preservation of the intestinal immune system" he stated, before he derailed once again talking about the provenance of the stolen Alexandrine, that costed the couple a fortune few years ago.

"May I ask where is the padlock? can we have it please? Thomas, can you take it..." Assistant Chief Constable Lowe talked while heading towards the front door.

"Professor Labutta we have finished now here. Everything is clear, we have all we needed". He really did not want to ask or know anything more, no matter what the Chief Superintendent would think about their report.

"It is here", Josephine answered, taking the intact shed's padlock from a shelf in the hallway and handing it over to PC Hardy who was ready to receive it, with the key still in its keyhole. She could clarify on the phone anything of her husband's statement if they needed it, she added. PC Hardy thanked her, and reassured his notes were absolutely exhaustive, then read the first paragraph of what would be their report: "Jon Thorn has, allegedly, deliberately trespassed using a passage in between the fences for the purpose of stealing six Alexandrine parakeets belonging to the Labuttas'. Is this right?"

"That's correct" Josephine concluded.

"Well, everything will be double-checked Mrs Labutta, do not worry" Lowe closed out: "Leave it with us. We will speak again with Mr Thorn but we have to go now. If there is anything else you want to put on file about last night you please give us a call again on 101 and quote the reference number. Thank you for the tea Madam".

He exchanged a compassionate glare with Josephine, while she kept the front door open for them.

On the doormat, Assistant Chief Constable Lowe felt he wasn't nervous anymore. At the end of the day, if the local police forces had to deal only with cases like this, London would be a safer town. He wanted to end the visit in a light tone, once again, congratulating the surgeon for his brilliant career, or at least that was his intention, regretting he had been anxious at the beginning of the visit. He realised even before he finished the sentence that his words would not be necessarily well received: "So you had a great time doing all those appendectomies back in the day.".

As a reaction, Labutta raised his voice once again, perhaps agitated by what the police officer might have alleged, that he wrongly, deliberately removed the appendix from so many people, knowing there could be alternative treatments: "How could we know that there is lymphoid tissue in the appendix? How could we imagine that this minimal organ has an important immunological function? Scientists thought the need for the appendix in the body was superseded by evolution. Superseded, not needed. We did not know there was an involvement of the microbiome. There was no idea of the gut microbiome at that time. Because it is composed of lymphatic tissue, it is indeed now recognised that the appendix must have some sort of immune function, but its purpose was never been understood during my time".

It seemed clear to Assistant Chief Constable Lowe that whatever was the type of mental health issue Professor Labutta was experiencing, he still had a lot of energy to lecture them for another hour. He exchanged a smile with PC Hardy, and the two almost run away, while the professor was still talking loudly in front of the house.

The elderly couple followed the two police officers towards their car.

Professor Labutta could not stop talking. His wife Josephine was holding his hand like he was a child she had just picked up from school.

References

- Girard-Madoux, M et al, *The immunological functions of the Appendix: An example of redundancy?* Seminars in Immunology, 2018, Volume 36, April, Pages 31-44
- Håkanson CA et al, *Childhood appendectomy and subsequent psychiatric illness*, PLOS Ment Health, 2025, 2(1): e0000219
- Kooij IA et al, *The immunology of the vermiform appendix: a review of the literature*, Clinical and Experimental Immunology, 2016, 186 (1): 1–9
- McDowell, J. and Windelspecht, M., *The lympthatic system*, Westport - London, Greenwood press, 2004
- Hu, X et al, *Alzheimer's disease and gut microbiota*, Sci China Life Sci October (2016) Vol.59 No.10
- Sago, S, *The functional landscape of the appendix microbiome under conditions of health and disease*, Gut Pathogens (2025) 17:38

The Missed Abortion

For months she called it the missed abortion: it was not recognised as a miscarriage but it was not an abortion neither. She couldn't talk about it openly, not even with the few friends who knew the truth, and insisted she should be seen by an haematologist. The least thing Ann wanted to do was to go back to the hospital: she knew she would not be taken seriously (1).

Nobody thought she should be assessed for Antiphospholipid syndrome, or any other blood disorder that might have caused the haemorrhage (2).

It was like Ann's body was trapped in a battlefield: doctors against nature, priests against God, blood without something, mother against love.

The pregnancy had come out of the blue. It was an accident. Ann would not make any family plan. And yet her entire life seemed taken over by the conceived: she was not in charge anymore.

In the end, everything converged on a deal: hadn't she always declared she did not want children? Now, this was a superimposed test. Suddenly, there wasn't a fetus to remove anymore, in spite of the appointment booked at the hospital. The embryo had just imploded entering the 8th week, leaving behind discarded cells, vestige of a colossal haemorrhage she melted into, in a car park, a late afternoon.

The doctor said she had to go to the hospital anyhow, to remove the scarred tissue. They would do that instead of the abortion, being the procedure pretty much the same.

Nobody wanted to investigate why it happened Ann had a miscarriage at the 8th week.

It seemed irrelevant she had a miscarriage in a pregnancy that she had not planned and she did not want.

What remained in the record was the abortion procedure at the 9th week. She felt like she was that bunch of scarred tissue. The denial of what had really happened to her body, to the essence of her own identity turned into an unstoppable flow of anxiety.

The miscarriage left Ann in a cage of sadness, with cognitive fog, for months. It shook the foundations of her identity, and self-reliance, with an inexplicable sense of inadequacy for not being able to carry on the pregnancy she did not actually want: she was not supposed to become a mother under any circumstances, no matter what she wanted.

Complete annihilation.

Ann's mother autistic coldness represented those contradictory torments. In spite of being present on her side all the way through, it was like she was just acting in a role of supervisor with a duty of care. Ann was her only soldier, left bleeding on a battlefield, and she had taken her to the extreme sacrifice of her sentient and emotional self, to an arguably needed abortion procedure. Because it had been booked!

The sense of isolation, the reprimand Ann felt around her, the toughness of the whole treatment, the emotional detachment of the nurses at the hospital, the indifference of the anaesthetist and the gynaecologist: everything was so surreal. It was like Ann did not rally exist. Only her body was there, reminding that a self-fulfilling prophecy had overrun the blood.

Fragments of the trauma, with the visual memory of the torrential haemorrhage that scared her to death, would impair any sexual desire, any feeling or thought about relationships for years.

However, with time it became clear she would never regret the decision to have an abortion. Her will had never been doubted, even by the mighty God or by nature: she did not want to have children, nor a family.

Ann recovered, slowly. For almost two years she studied for a vocational qualification while working every day, focussing on how to enter adulthood in a steady way, after that gigantic false start.

The following winter she decided it was time to go and live on her own. In this way, she began to put distance between herself and the perception of that poor body that had failed her.

Yet, many years later, she could not explain why the missed abortion drew such a sharp line between adolescence and adulthood, plunging her into an abyss of depressive thoughts, immense guilt for not being a mother, for not becoming a parent.

Weakened by smoking and infections that might have compromised her immune system, the recurrent bronchitis she suffered from for few years seemed to confirm it could have been impossible for her to be a mother, even in case she would have liked to do so.

Like the refrain of a song, every day from then on, she would hear a voice chanting the commitment that pulled her out of depression after the missed abortion: "*You are that child to live for*".

Notes

(1) Arya, S., et al, *"They don't really take my bleeds seriously": Barriers to care for women with inherited bleeding disorders*, Journal of Thrombosis and Haemostasis, 2021, 19(6), 1506–1514.

(2) The British Society for Haematology defines Antiphospholipid syndrome (APS) as "an autoimmune disease characterised by thrombosis (venous, arterial and/or microvascular) and/or pregnancy morbidity in association with persistently positive antiphospholipid antibodies (aPL)". The condition can occur in isolation or in association with other autoimmune diseases, typically Systemic Lupus Erythematosus (SLE) and rheumatoid arthritis. Guideline for diagnosis require a persistent (at least 12 weeks apart) presence of at least one biomarker in the blood and the occurrence of at least one clinical event (thrombotic and / or a pregnancy complication, usually a miscarriage). The condition is insidious and usually goes undetected until major thrombotic events occur. The exact dynamics that causes obstetric APS and loss of pregnancies are still debated with a wide range of circumstances. Also thrombocytopenia is a recurrent finding in people with APS. Treatment options are usually confined to anticoagulant and dual antiplatelet therapy (DAPT) for prevention of recurrent stroke. See also: Deepa J. Arachchillage et al, *Guidelines on the investigation and management of antiphospholipid syndrome*, Br J Haematol. 2024;205:855–880.

The Patch

It was the first appointment in the morning. Ann wanted the haircut done before going to work. The radio was covering the Space Shuttle Challenger disaster, making waves of sadness in the salon.

Kate, Ann's hairdresser since long, started trimming from the top. After less than a minute, she stepped back, almost jumping on her feet.

"What is this?", she squawked.

Ann looked up in the mirror: the hairdresser had on her face some degree of disbelief at something: "What?"

Perhaps the split ends? or that hairstyle was becoming inadequate for her dry, fragile hair? Or was Kate referring to the news of the seven poor astronauts disintegrated in the sky?

No, Kate was actually staring at her scalp with her mouth open: it was clear there was something odd exactly on top of Ann's head. She was incline to have a laugh though, waiting for the hairdresser to come up with something funny: "What?", she asked again. But this time around Kate just said gravely: "You have a hairless patch here. Why?"

Ann had no clue.

It was indeed Kate, the hairdresser, who discovered the hairless round shape at the back of Ann's scalp, the bald spot with no hair at all, large like a small orange, on the rear of the parietal bone, towards the occipital bone.

The hairdresser did not make any effort to conceal her astonishment. Like a vibe Kate's apprehension passed into Ann upper body, travelling from her fingers, still touching Ann's scalp, down through the neck and the shoulders of her young client.

Showing her the bald patch in a back mirror, Kate wanted to know if she was feeling alright, if there was anything awkward going on with her health that could explain that problem.

The fact that she had lost few inches of hair without being aware of it, without knowing, was something disturbing.

Few moments after seeing the patch in the mirror, Ann felt suddenly ashamed, and quite miserable. She hadn't had the time to notice she had a hairlessness teapot lid on top of her head, neither under the shower nor in front of the mirror: hurrying up the make up every morning, who would have thought she had to use a mirror to also look at the back of the head?

The fall in self-esteem and confidence was instantaneous and undeniable, even if she justified her mood at work with the sad news of the Challenger disaster that day.

She did not speak about the patch with anybody. If somebody asked her an explanation about it she would just simply say the bare truth and change subject: she was feeling perfectly fine and she did not know why she had lost hair in that strange way, but everything was under medical control.

She was not ill, she was not feeling tired, she loved to do many things at once, multitasking at work during the day and studying avidly in the evenings and during the weekends.

In sum, there was absolutely nothing to worry about. However, a little pandemonium in her finely organised daily routines was about to take over, and she knew it.

Where did this damn thing of hairlessness come from? Was she doing something or eating something wrong? Was she bursting energy at a pace incompatible with her circadian rhythms? The lack of sleep was indeed a problem from time to time, but otherwise she did not know how to answer those pressing questions.

Ann showcased her willpower with everybody for a couple of days, waiting to be seen by doctors: she did not want restlessness to ramp up from her legs, weakening her. So she tried to look buoyant as usual and simply sorted to say that the circular patch without hair on the skull was probably something due to the fragile nature of her natural hair.

The dermatologist who quickly saw Ann upon referral of her family doctor made the diagnosis: "it is a mild case of patchy alopecia aerata" (1), he proclaimed with a certain satisfaction. The specialist told Ann the problem was quite rare, the cause unknown, but it was nothing to be worried about: it may happen, for unexplained reasons, at any stage of life and to anybody, with stress considered the most likely culprit. It would heal in few months time on its own. Rest, going on holiday for few days, using some oily shampoos and moisturising creams would accelerate the recovery.

Alopecia is a type of skin dysfunction that lasts for few weeks or months and then resolves easily on its own, and it is unlikely that it returns, the consultant explained to Ann.

Sometimes it may indeed re-occur but in a lighter and different version, or with rosacea developing on the upper body. Do not panic: the general advice was to try to get into the habit of sleeping well and have a quieter life, drink a lot of water, and everything would be alright sooner than she feared.

The doctor was still talking to her when she started to figure out how to achieve a better work-life balance, what activities she had to reorganise, if there was something she could just get rid of.

There is no clear aetiology for alopecia: the dermatologist was keen to answer her question about the cause. But it seems that some people may be genetically predisposed to it. He did not suggest Ann should be tested for any autoimmunity problem or any allergy or intolerance: at that time, in 1986, the discovery of the autoimmune origin of alopecia areata was still long way off. The disease was considered a skin disorder, similar to eczema or atopic dermatitis.

Leaving the dermatologist's studio Ann phoned her mum to say there was nothing very serious to worry about and went back to work. For the rest of the day it was impossible not to ruminate about those two words: aetiology unknown.

She went on thinking about the dad of her friend Lea, who died a couple of weeks into the new year, one year before. A big man with the shoulders of a rugby player who suddenly became a tiny portion of himself because of a rare cancer that required a bone marrow transplant. He was the one and only other person Ann had ever seen with a bald round patch on the head similar to hers. Ann stayed the entire night of new year's eve at Lea's house, with her dad almost unconscious on the wheelchair. Few months earlier the poor man had had several operations and complications due to graft versus host disease (2). But in the meantime his hair had regrown a little bit, she had noticed, sinisterly, during the funeral service. For a second, she felt the irrational frightening, shivering thought that Lea's dad might have passed her a mysterious infection that was the real cause of alopecia areata.

What a nonsense fear of death disease brings to you, she talked to herself.

Day after day nothing seemed to happen to the patch.

Ann was told the recovery could be very slow but she could not bear the total absence of signs of hair regrowth. The silence of the patch inevitably caused a surge in anxiety. Contrary to what the dermatologist said, she became convinced that it would be unlikely for the hair to regrow there: she would remain forever obsessed with the image of a crater without hair on her head, a teapot without lid marking the skull.

On top of that, together with the bald patch, she experienced an unusual storm of sad feelings about everything.

Fatigue crept into her routines.

The patch was an utterly depressing nuisance to think about at all times, and try to hide at all times too. She had to admit that working and studying so many hours a day was perhaps the cause of too much stress, and poor sleep. Neither was healthy to always eat in a hurry: sandwiches, steaks and salads, or pastas and pizzas were not really healthy even if she avoided fried foods and excess of fats.

Ann had professional aspirations, academic goals, work engagements: suddenly, she saw excitement and passion fading away, day after day, demanding reserves of energy she did not have. For several weeks everything turned into dull, fatigued duties.

Reluctantly, but worried by the coincidence of losing hair and be challenged by feelings of depression and weakness, she went to talk with a psychotherapist.

"Apart from it, how is your health going, are you feeling well?", the counsellor asked.

The question slapped the air, like the baton of a conductor.

The noise of any other thought stopped. From somewhere inside, Ann dug out a surprising and clownish answer: "I may be a bit hypochondriac like my mother" Ann was saying, hearing a pinch, just a pinch, of humour in her own voice.

"Every now and then there is something about my health to be worried about, either my body urging attention, or medical exams to be done as soon as possible to confirm or exclude a disease - she continued -   but in fairness it has always been this way since I was little. So I have become used to it".

What a change of music for her own ears. She was saying, perhaps for the first time in her life, that her health was nothing like she was used to imagine and describe to herself, friends, colleagues and relatives: she was not at all a young woman fit and strong like a horse. Instead, very much like her mother, she had recurrent unknown short and long illnesses plus a bald patch of alopecia aereata of unknown aetiology had appeared on her skull, jeopardising everything.

Wasn't that the perfect portrait of an hypochondriac? was she saying she was like her mum? was she saying her own life was imprinted with her mother's pattern of idiopathic, or autoimmune,   health issues?

Every time she seemed remarkably well and everything was alright, her mum was used to phone and say that she had had an emergency or a spark of pain. Visits to A&E departments, medical consultations, interruptions, changes of programmes, of pace, of diet or something else would then follow: year after year, those flareups had become like a musical score, showing her mother's struggles, and tactics, in trying to get round new problems, very often considered of unknown or uncertain aetiology.

Exactly as it was now for Ann, dealing with this damned issue of alopecia areata and its consequences on her mood and stamina.

The counsellor did not discouraged Ann to further work on that chain of thoughts. Ann could see comic aspects in the entire family tale she was weaving, putting the matter on a more lighthearted, and yet perfectly sensible pathway: at the end of the day, if medicine does not have an answer or solution to problems, if science cannot explain what happens to our body, we'd better settle our mind on the most convenient consolations.

Ann's actual loss of hair could not be explained as hypochondria, the psychotherapist argued: there was nothing Ann had just imagined or feared. On the contrary, the rounded bald spot was there, and quite visible now she knew she had it: absolutely real, authentic, hairlessness.

However, the counsellor prepared her to make a gentle turn of attention, stepping back from her mother's foothold. Ann was not chasing any special attention by doctors, visiting specialist after after specialist, like her mother was used to do. On the contrary, Ann knew how to manage her own anxiety, that was perfectly normal in such a weird situation: going around with a shaved Olympic medal on the skull, displaying great nonchalance, come on... is not for everyone.

Strange symptoms happen in life: medics, as well as relatives, do not always have an answer to all the questions about health. If she had a more serious mental illness to worry about, instead of an obvious anxiety waiting for the hair to regrow, Ann could have considered first of all a wig, or the development of a pigtail, like the mythical Baron von Münchhausen who rescued himself and his horse from drowning, just lifting himself up by his own pigtail.

In sum, there was no much else to do, no other medical answer, than wait and see, and go on with her life in the meantime.

The chat, and the laugh, were really beneficial. Ann's anxiety slowly receded. After few weeks, tiny little hair appeared on the patch.

Touching them was like hugging an old friend after weeks of solitude.

Although she had several other unusual health issues in the following years, Ann did not experience any further episodes of alopecia areata.

She went on with her life, seeing how different she was, and wanted to be, from her mother, in spite of their genetic heritage and commonalities.

Ann could not imagine that the patch was just one of several juvenile manifestations of Sjögren's, a kaleidoscopic autoimmune disease causing several different dermatologic problems she was diagnosed only three decades later (4).

Notes

(1) Alopecia areata affects approximately 0.5-2% of the global population, according to Ho, CY et al, *Clinical and Genetic Aspects of Alopecia Areata: A Cutting Edge Review*, GENES Volume: 14 (2023) Issue: 7 (July) Article Number: 1362.

A molecular geneticist, Angela Christiano, inspired by her own lived experience, worked out in 2020 that several defective genes in the HLA region explain a predisposition to develop alopecia areata. The discovery was possible thanks to the analysis of data belonging to more than 5000 individuals.   See: *Autoimmune disease Outlook,* Nature Immunology, Vol 595, 15 July 2021, p. S56.

Further research into this condition over the last five years (2020-2025) demonstrated that alopecia areata develops with mechanisms closer to those seen in other autoimmune diseases, namely in rheumatoid arthritis, hyperthyroidism, Crohn's disease, vitiligo, psoriasis, lichen planus.

We now know that the cause of alopecia areata consists in what scientists describe as a collapse of the so called "immune privilege" that characterises hair follicles. These are thought to be unaccessible to immune cells, as minuscule spaces in the body in which there is no need for a special immune protection. The collapse of this privilege would mean, according to this theory, that the hair follicle starts signalling an abnormal state of danger with the consequence that immune T cells come along and attack it, causing the loss of hair. While in other cases of baldness and hairlessness the loss is permanent and the hair does not grow back, in alopecia areata the hair regrows after the flareup of the immune system has calmed down. This area of autoimmune symptoms and problems is currently under great scrutiny, experimentation and pressure from the big Pharma to develop treatments. For instance, new treatments for cutaneous autoimmune diseases based on Janus kinase (JAK) inhibitors are said in some scientific papers to being rapidly changing the management of conditions like alopecia, neutralising autoimmune dysfunctions and restoring skin health almost immediately. See also: Raychaudhuri, SP, *JAK inhibitor: Introduction,*   Indian Journal of Dermatology Venereology & Leprology, 2023 (89), 5, p 688-690; Silverberg, N, *The genetics of pediatric cutaneous autoimmunity: The sister diseases vitiligo and alopecia areata,* Clinics in dermatology,, 2022 (40), 4, p363-373.

(2) Bone marrow transplant is subject to many complications, due to the immune system rejecting the transplant tissues, the prevention of which can be managed through immunosuppressant drugs. Graft versus host disease is often fatal.

(3) The recent advances in understanding the autoimmune aetiology of alopecia areata have highlighted the need for a review of the so called psychogenic theory surrounding this as well as other skin conditions. See: Harries, M et al, *Epidemiology, management and the associated burden of mental health illness, atopic and autoimmune*

conditions, and common infections in alopecia areata: protocol for an observational study series,　BMJ OPEN, 2021 (11), 11, Article Number: e045718.

(4) Llamas-Molina, J.M.et al., *Localized Cutaneous Nodular Amyloidosis: A Specific Cutaneous Manifestation of Sjögren's Syndrome*, Int. J. Mol. Sci. 2023, 24, 7378.

The Gory Twins

"Jeffrey is a convicted pedophile. At 56 there is no way to save him from spending the rest of his life behind bars. It is a pain in the arse to even mention him again", Ron tried to explain. He learned to cope with the always stinging and throbbing memories his name brings back but Rose, his wife, says they have a poisonous mushroom in the family. She gets very agitated every time his name comes up.

"How did it start", asked the journalist investigating on behalf of Mitochondria Tomorrow, a research healthcare company working in partnership with a NHS trust.

"Who knows". That would be the end of the story.

Nobody knew Jeffrey had a double life.

The journalist wanted to dig out possible connections between genetic and paraphilic disorders. Instead of a study into biology or social science clues about mental, behavioural, neurodevelopmental disorders, Mitochondria Tomorrow wants to focus on real stories of patients. They selected few cases of convicted pedophiles with a complex medical history or a peculiar genetic heritage. It is a bottom up approach, she chanted over the phone. The story of two brothers, dizygotic, not identical twins, although with a remarkable physical resemblance, is an exceptionally interesting case, she pleaded. It is for the advancement of medicine: early diagnosis, preventative treatments, that type of noble purposes. By the way, Mitochondria Tomorrow obtained permissions from the Courts to access the whole medical history of the subjects identified by an AI algorithm through NHS records and other public domain materials. These cases, like Jeffrey and Ron's, are the most likely to provide relevant evidence and will be included in the study anyhow, anonymised.

It's a bit like saying he does not have a choice. He must collaborate in the attempt to make his views heard or correct inaccuracies in their family history that could also impact him, Rose and Lilly, his daughter. Everything he says would be treated strictly confidentially and anonymised, of course, and there will be a number of further options to protect his privacy and compensate his time or expense, the journalist assured.

"What the f..." Rose was furious at such news. She did not take it easy.
"You could tell them bullshit... for the advancement of science. a Court order? Mitochondria Tomorrow? how do you know these aren't crooks from the press?"
"She is a journalist with a strong reputation. She sent documents from the NHS trust too" Ron replied, unconvincing.
He did not want complications, on top of the hell they had gone through because of Jeffrey. It's just a couple of hours. So he texted back the journalist before dinner: it is alright to talk at the bar of the Churchill Hotel in North Lambeth, at half past five in a week time.

"Nobody knows what happened to him", Ron says, after a short introduction.
It seems the journalist is already aware that after graduation Jeffrey found a well paid job as a Radio presenter and DJ in the South West. Ron married Rose and had a daughter. Then the twins lost contact. The last time they met was before Jeffrey's trial, at mum's funeral, where it took one minute for them to agree to sell the family house and pay dad care home.
The journalist already knows a lot about their family life. She asks something hitting the nail on the head: "Tell me when you were both diagnosed with Bernard–Soulier syndrome (1), I think you where about to start secondary school, right?"
Ron has an incomprehensible knee-jerk reaction, like something has broken his rehearsed coolness. He answers with a shot of anger: "It was a misdiagnosis, for both of us". Then, like cataracts from hell, childhood memories submerse him.

Ron suffered from violent epistaxis (2) in his childhood and went through three cauterisation procedures, he says, and that was at the core of a long chain of medical consultations and exams that lasted several years, sometimes involving also Jeffrey, because doctors always wanted to check the twins together, until they were considered not anymore at risk of having a rare genetic blood disorder. Instead, what they experienced around the age of 15 or 16 were enormous carbuncles that sometimes needed surgery to drain, and did not heal easily without antibiotics.

"Interesting, tell me more: were these like big acne boils on the face? isn't it a frequent issue for teenagers to have acne? surely not as common as epistaxis...".

Ron pauses for a moment, he doesn't see what she wants to imply, at first. Rose's idea that the interview is another attempt of the press to exploit their family tragedy trumps on his patience. Perhaps his wife was right and he should have just said no.

Then his determination for an appeasement strategy to deal with the bizarre requests of the press or the NHS returns. He replies calmly.

"We were very different indeed, both in personality and in body reactions to irritants or infections... yes, carbuncles were big boils that appeared in the pelvic area, in the groin or under the armpits, not really like acne on the face".

Ron remembers a fistula that appeared on both his and Jeffrey's buttocks, pretty much on the same position, when they were about 12 or 13 years old. Jeffrey's required surgery for that, doctors had to cut its boil and drain it. Ron could avoid it as he obediently went through the administration of mercurochrome (3) as instructed by mum, even if it was quite scaring, and stinging. That was a powerful antiseptic available over the counter, effective in that: the big boil would dry out and recede in a couple of days. Jeffrey did not want it though. He was even used to laugh at Ron because the tincture left long lasting red stains on skin, fingers, his pants and sometimes also his trousers.

"It is a product that may have toxic consequences and it is not authorised anymore" the journalist comments.

"I guess so. Growing up, I do not remember I have seen it advertised or on chemists' shelves anymore. I still have every now and then a carbuncle developing but there are now lot of antibacterial products. I think also for Jeffrey the problem went on and on all the same over time".

"You said you were afraid of it? tell me more".

"I think it was just because it reminded me of blood, and the epistaxis".

Ron explains the epistaxis created in his mind as a child what is known as blood phobia: for long years, until he started work, every time he saw a drop of blood, including his own, he became dizzy. When he had to do blood tests, Ron always had to warn the phlebotomist: he could faint during or soon after. For Jeffrey that was always an opportunity to start bullying him. The third cauterisation was very effective, and solved his epistaxis problem once and for all. Conversely, the blood phobia remained. Sticky.

"Why was that?" the journalist asks, ordering two   bottles of tonic water.

Ron tries to relax while the interviewer digs into memories he would rather not to talk about: they do not seem pertinent in any way to Jeffrey's case.

Jeffrey went from the buoyant behaviour of a repressed gay adolescent to a sophisticated sociable, overt gay young man, in his early 20s, at a time in which homosexuality was still classified as a mental disorder. It was a very tough period.

How did it happen that he turned into a pedophile, chased by police, trialled and convicted with dreadful charges? Still today, it remains a mystery.

The journalist must have touched a chord, pulling back those visual memories of blood in their childhood. And it is not his own face that Ron remembers covered in blood on the doormat of their unfinished three-storeys family house in Dorset, at first.

Ron recalls they were 6 or 7 years old. He was running desperately down the road after hearing Jeffrey screaming. His brother had fallen off a bicycle they were riding downhill, in turn.

He must have stumbled somewhere. The whole neighbourhood was quite an unsafe place for children to play, because building work was ongoing everywhere, for the new town. But it was a vast playground too.

Ron found Jeffrey unconscious, laying in the middle of the road, covered in blood. His face unrecognisable. He picked his brother up and carried him in his arms back to the house, crying, shouting for help.

The way he recalls the incident is deeply touching, the journalist observes.

How did he find the strength to carry him, at that young age? they probably weight the same... Ron wondered that question too many times. He must have felt he had to fight for his own life bleeding out in his arms: it was his brother, that's all he can say.

Jeffrey's blood was pouring on Ron's shirt and shoes. Then he doesn't know what happened. He fainted on the doormat.

When Jeffrey returned home from the hospital, he had a long suture on his forehead. But he was smiling and mocking him as usual.

Who knows where he would be now if Ron had not run to him.

Yes, that idiot of Jeffrey, his twin brother, a convicted pedophile.

Not behind bars, perhaps.

"This is very interesting", is the journalist's comment, while she seems pondering something else, browsing nervously into her notebook with the Mitochondria Tomorrow logo on its cover. She wants to go back to the Bernard–Soulier syndrome, she wants to talk about the misdiagnosis now.

"So yours and Jeffrey's medical records were wrong? are they still containing errors in your opinion? I do not understand... what is that does not square here Ron?", she asks, seeming genuinely concerned she might have lot of unreliable data to sift through. "Why were you both diagnosed with a rare genetic condition, and then... this vanished from both yours and Jeffrey's medical record, few years later, when something else shows up, again..."

"I do not know, as I said it was an error but it is also true the body changes over time, you know", Ron reiterates, exhaling. There shouldn't be really anything to investigate anymore, in his opinion. The family doctor kept on file that note for some time. It was eventually deleted, probably after their parents divorced and they moved house.

His mum received a surprising NHS invitation for Ron and Jeffrey to go for a blood treatment, intravenous gamma globulin, while it had already been established they did not need any. She complained, the GP dealt with the issue, the records of the twins were amended after further blood tests, at least to the best of Ron's knowledge. However, memories of that period are quite confused in his mind. In secondary school the two brothers changed class, so they were not together anymore. They often went to doctors or see dad separately, from then onwards.

The journalist recaps what she has put down in the notebook: it was true that Ron, not Jeffrey, suffered from torrential nose-bleeding, or epistaxis, and blood phobia, and for some reason these were at first linked to a rare blood disorder the twins were both diagnosed with. However, this was recognised to be a misdiagnosis, for both, few years later. It is true that Jeffrey, who had a head impact incident at around the age of 7, did not have any nose bleeding or epistaxis problem. Since Ron and Jeffrey are not identical twins, could the doctors have hypothesised a family history of faulty genes, or a defective chromosome 17? Could this be at the root of the suspicion they had Bernard–Soulier syndrome? The journalist seems excited to have pinpointed something that would need more medical investigations, she says, but that is beyond her remit for now, almost talking to herself.

Ron would rather not add anything to those speculations: he remains silent for a while. If it is true that Mitochondria Tomorrow already accessed the whole of his and Jeffrey's medical records for research purposes, they probably already know, or they can quickly check, that in his 30s Ron was diagnosed, again, with a blood disorder besides another chronic, autoimmune disease (vasculitis). This time around they said he had immune thrombocytopenia, a coagulation defect that may perhaps explain also, in retrospect, his childhood epistaxis. He doesn't know if anything remotely of this kind happened to Jeffrey's too.

Better not to put more meat in the journalist's grinder. Ron leaves to her to drive the interview wherever she wants to, without adding any further stream of possible investigations.

"Nose bleeding in children is very common, you know... epistaxis can be exceptional events that happen for a variety of accidents" he comments, with a tone that is dismissive as much as hers is feverish.

"Was epistaxis the trigger of your blood phobia?" She rebuts, in her ding-dong, constantly conflating hypothesis and facts from the medical history of the two brothers, and jumping back and forth various factual issues, her own interpretations and medical notes from several GPs archives.

"Well, yes, very likely" Ron says. Apart from Jeffrey's bicycle incident, the indelible memory he associates with blood is the frightening torrent of jelly-like blood clumps engulfing his nostrils and throat. This is why he was so scared of nosebleeds, and bleeding in general.

Jeffrey did not have anything like that, neither he bruised or bled easily, he repeats for the second or third time.

They had lot of other unusual yet minimal issues in common, like the carbuncles, or not liking certain foods for instance, but Ron's epistaxis was nothing near anybody's else nose bleeding at his age, including his brother: the blood clots erupting from Ron's nose and throat were three to four centimetres long, and the flow of blood was unstoppable. That was the reason why various doctors sorted for cautery, not once but three times. Something awkward was happening in his young body for sure. Nobody could really explain why, nor give him a cure.

The unknown aetiology of recurrent epistaxis is called "blood dyscrasia" in textbooks of medicine, the journalist comments. It means a disorder of the blood.

"Yes", Ron knows and would like not to be lectured, anyhow. In fact, also his wife Rose wanted to know more about those haemorrhage episodes in Ron's childhood, after she read that epistaxis can be a sign of genetic diseases, rare conditions like hemorrhagiparous thrombocytic dystrophy, that damned very rare Bernard-Soulier Syndrome, the giant platelet syndrome, the immune thrombocytopenia and who knows what else (4). And so he spent long nights reading lot of medical textbooks and researching the internet to reassure her.

Something popped up as abnormal in his blood test results once again when he was 32, puzzling Ron's family doctor, the journalist reads from her notes.

Yes, Ron confirms that he recalls his GP at the time looking at the numbers that came from the lab with consternation: he could not explain why Ron had an abnormal number of giant platelets in the blood at that age. That could be helpful to detect thrombocytopenia once and for all, the journalist interrupts him. Yes, Ron confirms laconically, but he did not show any other symptom of that condition, so once again, the clinician excluded it. Once again he seemed to have lot of red herrings in his blood.

"When did it happened? It was at a stressed time?" she insists asking.

"Well, yes, probably it was a stressful time", Ron concedes. It was a busy time, with Rose pregnant, and he had just started a new job. He could not care less if he had giant platelets for unknown reasons. He was feeling good. Apparently, the count of the giant platelets in the blood (needed for a diagnosis of thrombocytopenia) requires special attention by lab technicians because these molecules can be mistaken for lymphocytes in automatic counters (5), the journalist explains, and perhaps also the opposite is true.

So, once again, he might have gone through another misdiagnosis... She stares at him, then like talking to herself once again, takes notes.

Ron shrugs, not seeing how can she draw a connection with Jeffrey's case on the grounds of these hypothesis, or about Ron's medical record, once clarified they were dizygotic twins and had very different lives by the age of 20, when Jeffrey's pedophile life has already started, far away from the family house, according to his proceedings.

The journalist recaps once again to make sure she does not mess up her notes: the Bernard-Soulier syndrome was misdiagnosed for the brothers in their childhood, the epistaxis problem Ron suffered as a child was sorted through cautery, nothing to do with Jeffrey's hospitalisation after a bad head impact incident when he also lost a lot of blood, and as far as the giant platelet count is concerned Ron encountered this in his 30s, just in one occasion, treated as a red herring. By the time of this last issue, Ron and Jeffrey had lost contact singe long. Ron does not remember Jeffrey ever telling him of suffering of anything with his blood.

"Correct", he closes.

"Tell me more about the operation, the cautery, if you would", she orders tea for two to a waiter.

That was the solution to Ron's real problem. Today cauterisation can be executed as an outpatient procedure. Back in the late 1960s it was not so common. It required hospitalisation. He had to go through it three times between the age of 9 and 12. Luckily enough, the third time was the resolutive one, performed under total anaesthesia in a new hospital. It followed a quite dramatic episode that happened while he was at school, and yes, in that occasion Jeffrey was with him. They were in the same class that year, same teacher, same clothes.

The torrential nose bleeding contained clumps of bloods larger than his mouth. The blood clots were pouring violently from Ron's nostrils. Other clumps would bounce out from his mouth with spasms involving the whole upper body: he had to spit and not to swallow the clumps, somebody shouted at him, but nobody gave him instructions on how to deal with the sense of suffocation. Something that he will never forget.

The visual memory of those epistaxis haunted him for years.

However, by the age of 16, seeing blood and coagulated blood did not trigger any fainting feeling anymore: a sense of passing out while seeing blood had completely gone after spending almost three weeks in the department of the local hospital.

Ron's mother insisted he should be kept in isolation, fearing he had an infective form of hepatitis that could be passed to Jeffrey. It was another obscure period in his adolescence: he does not recall anybody coming to visit him. He had blood tests every day over there, and transfusions too, so he got desensitised, used to the idea that blood was to be considered just a substance, like milk or orange juice.

Nobody went to visit him while isolated for hepatitis? Once again, the journalist seems to hint at his role in the family as a possible neglect, compared to Jeffrey's. She wants to go back again to Jeffrey's incident with the bicycle when they were little, when Ron might have saved Jeffrey's life, preventing him to die by exsanguination.

Jeffrey's might have suffered from a brain injury because of the concussion?

There isn't much else to say or imagine, Ron says, exhaling once again, but yes in theory it is possible that Jeffrey suffered a traumatic brain injury in that occasion. It was a violent impact that left a two or three inches scar on his forehead.

They lived in that big semi-detached three-storey house at the time, until their parents divorced few years later: building work was ongoing at all times.

Everybody was building houses that would never be really finished. It was one of those things of the 1960s. Kids were used to play every day in an environment that today would be considered unsuitable: bonfires of waste lighted in the backyards, cement dust, welding fumes. Those sorts of things that today are very much looked into in relation to climate change and allergies. The air in all the spaces used for allotments, gardens and greens was saturated with pollutants, not less than the streets and lanes jumbled with vehicles. Is there any connection between that type of environment and the risk of developing blood disorders? He might have been exposed to some substance that irritated him up to the point of rupture of the tiny blood vessels in the anterior region of the nose called Kiesselbach's plexus or Little's area (6) and then the problem became chronic.

A disruptive domino effect in the vessels of his nose could have been the very reason of his epistaxis, is the journalist's verdict. She talks with the overconfidence typical of certain science writers, but Ron does not want to argue, he just shrugs once more: at the end of the day it may be a problem for Mitochondria Tomorrow, not for him, to explain with certainty the cause of his blood issues, and why Jeffrey's did not have any.

Ron reiterates he does not know. While Rose was pregnant it turned out he might have had, once again, a rare, and difficult to diagnose with certainty, blood disorder: so he searched databases of clinical literature on the internet, went to talk with specialists trying to understand more. It was unclear if it was a genetic condition or not. At the same time his twin brother was investigated and incarcerated as a pedophile, a scandal crumbled upon him and his family, and this time around he had a pregnant wife too. He just froze. He started thinking to the coming baby as the only purpose of his life, minute by minute.

"I understand", the journalist says. "Who does want to have a pedophile as family member, while waiting for a new baby? So the mystery of your possible coming and going blood disorder remained unsolved".

"Yes, something like that" Ron confirms. Doctors did not come up with anything but the reassurance that her daughter was perfectly fine. And his own blood tests turned out to be normal too after Lilly's birth. So, he would like to shout now, what's the point of being tormented with his interview now - or is it an interrogation?

The journalist retreats on Ron's catastrophic epistaxis, asking if he can please go back to his childhood: does he remember when it was the last one?

He does: it was just before his 12th birthday, late May, at school.

Ron can vividly recall the faces of some of his classmates, terrified like he was, and the teacher, so alarmed, who called the ambulance. He was horrified by the amass of jelly clumps of blood gurgling into his throat and then propelling out into the handkerchief, the coat, a big towel somebody had given to him. The torrent of blood had never been so gory. A crowd of pupils surrounded him while he was told to lie down on the floor of the school corridor. Yes, Jeffrey was there too, they were still in the same class.

Then Ron fainted and stayed in and out of consciousness until he saw the face of a surgeon, amid the strong lights inside the operating theatre at the hospital.

Somebody was whispering into his ears. Perhaps it was Jeffrey.

The convalescence after this third definitive cautery was long: he would go around for days with cotton pads in his nostrils, breathing with his mouth open. Jeffrey was bullying him with stories of vampires.

There was something unusual in Jeffrey's ostentation of masculinity and emotional detachment at that age, especially considering his homosexuality, the journalist notes, one would have expected him to be more sensitive?

Ron does not have anything to add on this point, but he could talk about his own epistaxis for ages, if this helps.

"Jeffrey's personality is something the press has already investigated inside out", he says, tired. Then Ron starts talking very quickly, repeating himself, in the hope she also accelerates on whatever she's trying to reckon or discover.

When the cotton pads were eventually removed, he continues, he was left with a long-lasting sensation of a smelly nose: the blood clumps had gone, but a persistent metallic taste had settled in. Perhaps the cauterisation changed something in the olfactory receptors that would turn into smell dysfunction many years later. Still today, when it happens that his nose bleeds for just a second, because of a cold or a too vigorous blow of his nose, Ron's whole body gets an imperceptible shake, a lash on hidden tiny nerves lasting milliseconds but enough to recall the smell and taste of blood, he says. It happens very rarely but his heartbeat still tumbles down, and then speeds up in a roller coaster. The arrhythmia goes away quite soon leaving him with fatigue, and flashing visual memories of himself vomiting blood clumps, or carrying Jeffrey in his arms, again.

In sum, plenty of blood all the way, he tries to leverage on some residual sense of humour as he would really like to end the interview and not to be asked again and again the same questions. He cannot be 100% sure about anything in relation to Jeffrey but very likely his twin brother has never suffered from any blood issue. Full stop.

"Do you remember when your epistaxis started?" the journalist seems asking questions in a rondo: when he thinks the interview is eventually over, or at least a certain chain of questions is exhausted, she recommences everything again. It is exhausting. Does she want to test him somehow? Is that a technique used for police interviews, and not for genuine medical research purposes? Is this journalist a covert criminologist, or a psychiatrist? Ron asks himself. Then, reluctantly, he sits back and opens again his box of memories.

"I think it was pretty much at the same time of Jeffrey's incident with the bike" he says.
The journalist says that as far as she knows epistaxis might have been due to a lesion in his septum caused by impact, for instance a fall. Or perhaps a slap across the face, she hints.
Yes, Ron confirms: he and Jeffrey were often subject to harsh physical punishments from both their parents, each with a peculiar style, but it was Ron to pay that price, most of the times. The robustness of the slaps sometimes left black and blue marks on his face: those were signs of her father's hands. Her mother suffered from tantrums of severe depression that she seemed to overcome only by way of turning aggressively towards other family members. She had a range of ways to physically assault him, during attacks of rage in which she threw everything up in the air, or against him and his father, while Jeffrey was often on the run on his own or with his friends.
Ron looks into the journalist's eyes before continuing, just to see if she really wants to go into those dark memories, not really pertinent to Jeffrey's case, that are not even mentioned in their medical records. Perhaps this is what she really wants? Would those particulars ever be helpful to explain what happened to Jeffrey's mind? why did his twin brother start chasing children?
He remembers in particular one occasion in which his mother jumped on him like a big feline, a ferocious animal. Ron run in his bedroom, where Jeffrey was hiding under the bed. "She was able to reach me there and bit me on my arms, neck, and cheeks, leaving bruises and black and blue marks that teachers, mum's colleagues, would pretend not to see for weeks", Ron recollects.

"Jeffrey's was laughing at that cruelty inflicted on me" he adds plainly and calmly after a little pause. "However I do not think I had any nosebleed after those slaps or assaults" he concludes firmly.

"My father?" Ron needs to think about him for a moment.

"He was a man very distant from everything, even before the divorce. He always wanted me to avoid any nose-picking, as many kids do, worried about the excess of crusting and scabs. Those dry bits and pieces in my nostrils were annoying my breathing. Even the sea water most of the times would not be beneficial. My dad encouraged nasal washing with clean sea water, and that remedy seemed quite effective. For some years he stored tanks of sea water collected during the summer holidays by the sea, and kept it in the basement. I would use it for nasal washing during the winter months, when visits to the beaches were less frequent. At some point Jeffrey decided to urinate inside the tanks, and he did not get any punishment for that. Mother laughed, and my nose washes just stopped".

Ron finishes his glass of tonic water. The journalist remains speechless and turns to her glass too, as the tea is over. She surprisingly announces that she has no more questions. Then, while they are standing by the counter, where she wants to pay the drinks: "It is weird you are twin brothers but so different from each other, how do you explain it?" she asks.

He is exhausted, and fears the journalist wants to recommence with questions, or she may want a follow up. It is a very stupid question to ask, in the end. Perhaps Rose was right.

"We are not identical twins" he just says, bitterly.

She shows she understood it is really time out: she thanks him, saying his testimony would be very appreciated by the research team at Mitochondria Tomorrow, leaning forward with her right arm and hand.

Ron smirks at her, rushing towards the revolving door of the hotel, leaving without the handshaking she was expecting.

Notes

(1) Orpha.net (by the French National Institute for Health and Medical Research) and StatsPerl (by the USA National Library of Medicine) have concise and up to date web pages presenting data and essential references about Bernard-Soulier syndrome, a complex blood

disorders, difficult to diagnose, that can be immune mediated, acquired in the context of other diseases or determined by genetic predisposition.

(2) Law, J., & Martin, E. (Eds.), *Concise Medical Dictionary*, Oxford University Press, 2020 reads that epistaxis "can be caused by low-grade bacterial infection of the front of the nose, hypertension, clotting disorders, or tumours of the nose or sinuses. Treatments include pinching the bottom part of the nostrils together, cauterising the bleeding vessel, or packing the nose with preformed packs, antiseptic gauze, or specially designed inflatable balloons. Occasionally surgery is required to interrupt the flow of blood to the nose". Few investigations available about the association between autoimmunity and epistaxis remain inconclusive. Clinical literature reports very rare cases of sever haemorrhagic episodes and nose bleeding in people affected by Lupus (SLE), Hughes (another name for antiphospholipid syndrome) or Vasculitis as well as people exposed to occupational hazards in the construction industry in Western countries. Similarly, researchers have hypothesised explicitly in recent years that various systemic conditions (in particular antiphospholipid syndrome) may be considered the cause of nasal septal perforations and other lesions to the nasal vessels. These may also result in acute or chronic episodes of epistaxis. See: Roca B., *Epistaxis y enfermedad sistémica (Epistaxis and systemic disease)*. Acta Otorrinolaringol Esp. 2009 Nov-Dec;60(6):456-8.

Other routes of investigations that link unusually severe cases of epistaxis to autoimmune diseases point to inflammatory and allergic reactions. See for instance: Murthy P, Laing MR. *An unusual, severe adverse reaction to silver nitrate cautery for epistaxis in an immunocompromised patient*, Rhinology. 1996 Sep;34(3):186-7; Yau S. An update on epistaxis. Aust Fam Physician. 2015 Sep;44(9):653-6. More information on this disorder are available through the Orphanet database, in the section about the condition coded with number 274.

(3) Merbromin, mostly known with the brand name of Mercurochrome, was banned in the USA and several other western countries in the 1990s because of potential mercury toxicity on skin and wounds.

(4) The NHLB Institute of the US NHI, the BMJ, Mayo Clinic, John's Hopkins and other online popular resources have disclosed or updated in recent years the available knowledge about immune

thrombocytopenia. For a more general overview of the complexity of diagnosis of these conditions, aimed at medical students and specialists, see: White, GC, *Congenital and acquired platelet disorders:current dilemmas and treatment strategies*, Seminars in Hematology, 2006 (43), January, Supplement 1:S37-41.

(5) Handin, RJ, *Inherited platelet disorders*, Hematology, 2005, 1, 396-492. The protocols in use for differential diagnosis vary greatly among countries. Family members who are carrier of Bernard-Soulier syndrome are often asymptomatic and with normal platelet counts. Reported in literature are also cases of horrible consequences of misdiagnosis, including splenectomies, intravenous and other life-changing treatments. In patients with a genetic condition the platelet transfusion may provoke an immune adverse response. See also: Lanza, F., *Bernard-Soulier syndrome*, in Orphanet Journal of Rare Diseases 2006, 1:46.

(6) Tiny blood vessels in the anterior region of the nose called Kiesselbach's plexus or Little's area take the name from the surgeons that discovered this as a precise point in the nose the frailty of which is considered one the causes of recurrent nosebleed. The nasal cavities are covered with a layer of soft tissue or membranes that wrap tiny blood vessels like a layer of clingfilm: both membranes and blood vessels can be scratched and broken due to inflammation and irritants in a wide range of situations. Frequent colds, sneezing, robustly blowing the nose, nose-picking, intense stress, and injuries are among the complications the tiny blood vessels in the nose of a child may go through. Through the nostrils irritants, inhaled ashes and dust particles, smoke of cigarettes, pollutants from exhausted vehicles, allergens, viruses and nasty bacteria can enter the body. The nerve endings in the nostrils cannot get easily rid of unwanted substances or the scabs that build up from mucus than does not drain properly, as well as dust and dry air: they just get inflamed and swell. All in all, the only way the body can eliminate irritant particles trapped into mucus may consists in expelling them explosively, with sneezes or sudden episodes of whooping cough or rupture of capillaries.

Penicillin Power

1

Very punctual as usual, Marion sent her an email with the transcription to review, inclusive of detailed instructions reminding rules, symbols, marks to use. The producer had already gone through all this on the day at the Health Documentaries' office: Rose should provide a digital signature too, agreeing (again) all the terms and conditions of her participation to the co-creative programme.

Marion warned her the company had these strict procedures to be certain every participant was happy with the contents they would pass to the Director: Health Documentaries had a record of zero claims or complaints about personal data in over two decades history of market research and successful films, in a niche where they almost had no competitors.

It would take Rose little extra time to review what she said during the individual interview, in addition to the day she already spent at the studio, in exchange for an additional payment of 25£ if everything was fine. If not, or in case of issues that would require complex legal or editorial considerations, she would receive the payment all the same but her testimony could be either put on hold or completely erased. It was convenient for the company to operate such a policy to save on legal costs and potential litigations, retaining creative ideas and even anonymised contributions, without any infringement of copyright or privacy law, of course.

Rose was not used to all those precautions, checks and balances, terms and conditions, advance notices, strict procedures. She started to read the transcription of her filmed interview. She recognised her answers but after few paragraphs she stopped, slightly confused, and texted Marion: "There are no questions, is this right? did you forget anything?"

All good, Marion replied swiftly, it was specified in the engagement blue-sheet. The Director may change the wording of the questions, or decide to use a non linear narrative, as he reserves the right to make big changes while editing the contents also minutes before the final cut of the film.

Rose began understanding her friend workplace culture, eventually: another participant told her this director, many years ago, at the beginning of his career, had worked with Peter Weiss, a famous exponent of the so called Theatre of Fact. Rose vaguely remembered she must have at least read that name in one of her university courses but nowadays it sounded more as a sort of ancestor genre of reality tv productions. At Health Documentaries, producers and directors wanted to collate and work creatively with the different voices: they would adjust the questions to make sure that words of patients and experts, Marion explained, would fit nicely in the assembly of the film. Rose would like to say she is very familiar with issues of assembly of characters, scenes and ideas but she wouldn't give 100% approval in advance for her words to be put in a context she did not know anything about. Then trust and gratitude for her friend prevailed, as she did not want to make any trouble to Marion for just this minimal job, and it wasn't her own script they were talking about after all. So she went on and read some of the transcription for the second time, caring for actually reviewing her words this time and not the architecture and organisation of work at Health Documentaries (that was none of her business):

(...)

I remember the little penicillin powder bottle my parents were used to carry with us everywhere. How did it start... Well, impossible to say with certainty. The 1960s and 1970s were years of great enthusiasm for the medicine that was still new for us: perhaps they over-learned the lesson that penicillin saves lives. They always had with them the little bottle with that genie cure inside... it was simple to carry around... Beige, puffy, with a green or brown lid. The content vaguely resembled talcum powder. It seemed just a magic solution to me... I suppose I liked the idea of a supernatural remedy coming to rescue me: sprinkled over any wound, it would ease the itching, stop the bruises from bleeding, exterminate the pus, you know... it WAS magic.
(...)
Yes, I was prone to bruises. Every now and then there were minimal red drops of blood on my clothes, trails of blood in the house... impossible to hide the fact I was so prone to bleeding for nothing,

really.... Often it started with just a minuscule, apparently insignificant crack in the skin of my legs, a little cut on my knees, a scratch on my arms. Many children of my age had similar experiences though, so it did not worry me nor, I think, my parents, at least until a certain age, when it was clear the frequency of my little bruises was not that normal...

(...)

I can't remember honestly. Bruising episodes were annoying every few days, probably weekly? I was just given the genie powder of penicillin every now and then, probably at least once or twice a week.

(...)

I was feeling... guilty, I suppose. For I was giving trouble to my parents, especially while we were travelling or going on holiday....you know, we had to stop and do the medication, my bruises always being object of attention...

At the first sign of bruises they would stop the car or whatever they were doing and shout "hurry up, the powder". So perhaps that is the reason why I remember the little bottles so well (laugh)

(...)

I've often thought there may be a connection. I did not know anything about the hygiene hypothesis of autoimmune diseases but perhaps in the mid 1960s there wasn't awareness of it? Now it is easy to see that perhaps Penicillin was given too often... Perhaps it was like using a tanker to flat a mosquito? (laugh) As far as I can remember there were no concerns about possible misuse or excessive use of topic antibiotics...

(...)

No, I have not developed any antibiotics resistance as far as I know. I still have a very sensitive skin though, I have Lupus...

(...)

It is almost silent or latent but from time to time I have a bad rash or some other signs of a flareup... diagnosed after I struggled to get rid and recover from a chickenpox infection, that was I was told might have triggered SLE... I may also have other autoimmune conditions...

(...)

Yes, I was a teenager, diagnosed when I was 15 or 16....Anyhow my skin still cracks and at times peels easily. I spent much of my teenager years with frequent bacterial infections, rushes, bruises on limbs, hands, fingers... Still today skin problems are the most annoying

symptom.... Large spectrum antibiotics always work well with me...
you know, skin and soft tissue infections can also spread easily to
joints and the blood in my case... In a flare, when my immune system
overreacts to something, the only thing that really saves me, that
placates the spasms of an inflamed spleen or kidney is a course of
antibiotics. Full stop. No matter what it may be the real cause of the
threat - or if there is any threat at all - I feel lucky I have some
awareness of how these flareups starts, how to avoid them as much as
possible and I have also understood empirically how it can end ...
(...)
Dependence may be a too strong word. Honestly I do not believe I
have developed any sort of dependence on any medication, including
antibiotics, but since the time of the beige vintage bottle of penicillin
powder it is true that I rely on antibiotics... when I see my skin
bleeding I do think immediately I have to take immediate action to
prevent an infection .... perhaps just a plaster most of the time, but I
do have to be much more careful... in many occasions I had to take
antibiotics for what seemed at first a stupid infection on my thumb...
(...)

2

Few days after that text of the interview to be reviewed without the
questions, Marion sent Rose via email the link to another customer
satisfaction questionnaire, this time asking her to rate the experience
of working with Health Documentaries Ltd.
It was part of their standard procedures, Marion explained when Rose
texted her to object she had worked only one day for their co-creative
pre-production programme and did not have much feedback to share
on "working with Health Documentaries".
"Just please answer the questionnaire Rose, it takes only two minutes"
Marion cut shortly.
Then she texted Rose on her mobile number: "Please do not say we
went to the same primary school. (emoticon)"
"Ah ah", Rose texted back "I knew it, you do not want me to say I am
your mole at work. (emoticon)".
Marion was her only friend at this difficult time, and she had been
very helpful.
Rose filled the feedback questionnaire, adding sincere suggestions for
improvements and comments: she found awkward, for instance, that

in the age of AI there were still need to focus groups in person, people interviewed face to face, for the purpose of developing a narrative for a medical documentary. But all in all she really had a positive experience. She found the whole machinery of the co-creative pre-production survey fascinating: the organisation of everything to obtain original user generated contents, but in a highly controlled way, was curated in any minimal detail. Her friend Marion was brilliant: she was so proud of her friend professionalism. Nonetheless, there was something bitter: everything seemed somehow rudimental and chilled compared to the faster, exciting and chaotic organisational settings she was used to work for. Video games teams are probably more agile than documentary film productions, Rose thought. For a moment, after she clicked the button "submit" at the end of the customer satisfaction questionnaire, she felt her pulsations plunging. A sensation of cold was invading any inch of her skin, any vibe.

She really missed her job, a career she had studied and worked for so hard for years.

The idea that her reputation had vanished because a man decided to harass and slander her saying he had an affair with her was breathtaking, still unbearable.

3

Rose had made giant steps as a game designer in the fast-paced, male dominated industry of video games. But after she accidentally flirted with a client, Brian Morris, or allegedly so, at the New Year's party, things have changed dramatically quickly for her.

She worked in the same company for almost seven years. Outstandingly creative, she was much appreciated for a rare combination of skills, hands-on sensitivity, never missing a deadline. She grew up in the sector, as an apprentice, then a graduate.

At times, she could be judged naive in her views about current affairs, or expressing comments about colleagues' behaviours: she often gave the impression of living in a parallel world, fuelled with fantasies she had been cultivating since long. That explained both her social awkwardness and her talent, for which she was admired but also, occasionally, looked down by snob, more experienced colleagues, or labelled as "on the autistic spectrum disorder" even if she was very good at communicating with others.

Things precipitated in the spring, after Brian Morris approached Rose during a press conference for the release of a new game. Morris wanted her to go in the cloakroom with him. Furthermore, Rose rejected his advances around the buffet, and purposely dropped a mayonnaise filled canapé on his trousers, while saying bitterly to him: "Watch your step Brian: you are being a great nuisance to me.". He laughed at her, and that laughing sounded hysterical and vindictive at once: he wasn't laughing with amusement or for a sense of relief. He was laughing in disbelief that she could be so confrontational.

Morris did not stop there. He sent her text messages saying he was in love with her, that theirs was more than an affair. It was a mockery, but why her? What was the purpose of it?

Affair? She was horrified. What the hell was going on in his mind?

She kept deleting Morris' messages in the hope they would just stop coming. They did not.

Morris even tried to lure her into saying they were "in a relationship" in front of her colleagues, at the end of a briefing meeting. Everybody laughed but then they looked at her with mixed admiration and prudery, as it could be true she was in a relationship with the client.

This could be the start of a slanderous campaign to include in the plot for a video game, if I was the game character, she thought. But a sense of respect for her own identity and sanity prevailed: This must be stopped. This could not go ahead.

She resolved it was urgent to speak with the person she trusted more in the company, her manager John.

Rose thought John should, and could, take action, talking with the legal department. She said Morris had been acting as a drunkard maniac for few months, making unwanted sexual advances.

John was surprised. "I am very sorry to hear Rose but I thought you were genuinely very close, I did not know how much but... that was the general impression I had for some time, that the two of you might have seen each other at some point and that was not necessarily a romance, you know, it is not my business and the company does not have strict policies in place about these things", he said.

"Absolutely no" Rose palpitations boomed. She said everything started in January. She had an accidental flirtation episode with Morris at their New Year's party, when they had too much wine, and everybody was wandering around, kissing and hugging everybody else, as he may remember. Even in that occasion there was no sexual intercourse or anything like that, only some casual petting of two drunk people, after she stumbled on a pile of suitcases in the cloakroom, looking for her coat: Morris came along for some reason and fell on her, or perhaps he did it on purpose... So they ended for some time on the floor, laughing and touching each other "inappropriately" she would say: it must have been ten minutes or the like, until someone else came along, or they got distracted. She remembers that she found her coat and went home. He might have had an hallucination moment? Since then he has been a pest with Rose for almost four months.

"Oh dear" John did not know what to say, genuinely surprised and embarrassed to hear that sort of confession. Filling her a glass of water, he said the whole thing seemed totally absurd to him but of course he believed her and wanted to *sort the friction out*. As far as John knew, Morris had a very stable relationship with a blonde financial broker, he saw the couple few nights ago at a Charity dinner. So... it sounded out of Brian's jovial character that he engaged in harassing behaviour, even in public, persistently. More likely is that Brian felt a special, lighthearted yet professional fondness for her, nothing to be worried about, or at least this is what John imagines their important client would say if poked about the two of them. However he would do everything he could to help Rose regaining her confidence, piece of mind at work and beyond and not to be bothered any further, of course.

John asked if Rose had any evidence they could put forward to the legal department, for an initial assessment of the situation, to see what should be done, in case they wanted to go that route: being Morris one of their biggest clients they had to proceed with extreme caution. Rose said that for that same reason, to protect the client as much as herself while in extreme distress, she always cancelled from her phone text messages and pictures Morris had sent to her, including the most peculiarly dreadful and offensive evidence: he had exposed himself with photos while he was in the company's toilet, and sent at least two dozens of harassing texts in which he even suggested Rose could go with him in their meeting room and perform sexual acts on him.

John invited her not to delete anything Morris would send to her phone or mailbox from that moment onwards and reassured her: "You have been heard Rose".

A couple of weeks passed. Morris did not send any further photo or messages. Rose reported to John few more oddities, trusting once again she would be believed, and supported. The fact that Morris was waiting for her to leave the office, hiding in a black cab, then following her walking back home, shouting from the car "Rose please get in the cab, we need to talk" or "Rose can I come to your place tonight?" were not enough to substantiate any legal involvement or accusation of harassment. John told Rose he could not discuss anything of that kind with the legal office without risking his job.

He concluded: "Just ignore him, forget him, he might have had a true moment of madness, you know... these things happen".

Rose became very agitated. For the first time in her life she lost a file, something she had been working on for over one month. It seemed people were kind with her, but mostly did not want to talk with her. She felt she was being mobbed.

She tried, in vain, to explain to John again that Morris' fixation and torment was causing her a huge distress, she could not work and sleep peacefully anymore. The team was isolating her. Morris had found subtle ways to constantly harass her, reminding her his menace and molestation in ways people would judge funny or innocuous, such as making calls for her through the reception that would announce him seconds before he would run to the exit saying "Tell her I am waiting for her in the taxi outside".

Rose had a bad flareup and had to take a couple of days off. Morris sent her flowers with a boy that buzzed her phone asking for a "Mrs Rose Morris?".

She asked to speak with the Human Resources and the Corporate Affairs departments. He must be told to stop. She trusted her employer would protect her. That was not in the plot, evidently: to put out the fire, the company chose another way. She was told her current main project was decommissioned out of the blue, some other stuff she was working on passed to others. Big changes ahead required a quick agile reorganisation. She was sacked.

Relatives and friends found impossible to believe that out of the blue Rose had lost her job because of a "difference of opinion" with the management, that was the official version. There must have been something else.

She cried in despair for not less than six hours a day for a fortnight, that transformed her face in a copper-coloured colander, with the occasional flush of a reddish-yellowish firefly on cheeks and nose. Everybody was saying she had gone mad, John said around she had a serious mental health crisis and that was due to her Lupus disease - that was utterly untrue.

"Cheap gossiping", her friend Marion texted her. "Stay strong".

The rheumatology clinic kept her busy for a while.

Finding herself without a job has come as a shock. Without the daily reminders of the cozy network of relationships with her colleagues, most of whom had known her as university mates, feelings of isolation set upon her even further, as the heavy black clouds of a storm after a terrible summer.

The phone was mute.

She tried for some time to talk to people in position of power that knew her, with the idea she could be given the chance to explain what had really happened to her, at least by those who had praised her in the past, publicly or privately. Nobody was interested or available to take her calls. Only nasty recruitment algorithms would reject her applications.

Then she retracted, like an injured dog, and stayed for long hours at home listening to jazz music and financial news as she was living on another planet, without almost no interactions.

Eczema and some purulent papules took over all over the body, reminding her she had a terrible disease. Time to take her usual course of large spectrum antibiotics and really go and ask for help.

4

Marion, her friend working as assistant producer, came to the rescue, offering the paid engagement for that panel she was organising for the next film by an important director they usually worked with. Health Documentaries Ltd produced mainly co-creative documentaries. For this one, the producer and the director agreed to recruit a mixed cast of medics and patients with a diagnosis of autoimmune disease.

"Rose you are the perfect candidate", Marion said trying to infuse some enthusiasm, and swore there was no favouritism on her side, as she truly believed what she said.

In particular, the film would   review the hygiene hypothesis of autoimmunity (1), that could also be of some interest for her. The director wanted to make a documentary that would be offered not only through streaming services but also in community settings and schools, as there aren't many on the subject and the only one in circulation dates back to 2001 (2).

"Rose you have nothing to lose, it is just one day and you will be paid quite well", Marion insisted "come and do something different, you need to move forward, stop filling all those jobs application forms Rose, you need to bounce back at some point".

Reluctantly, Rose accepted Marion's offer. Everything had been smoothly organised: coffee-breaks, lunch, free time to chat with other members of the panel that comprised two groups - the patients and the medics - and Marion was affable with everybody.

It was like having a good coldish shower after a long walk in a heatwave: Rose had almost forgotten how nice can be life when people work with other human beings, humanely.

The producer, an Irish tall middle-age man with orange hair and relaxed but sad look, spent at least half an hour to introduce their methodology and project, very professionally. Part of the contents they would discuss were or could be perceived as having a personal, sensitive nature, he said unfolding the agenda for the day, so that Health Documentaries would rather assure that the transcription of everything each participant would say during the interviews and then throughout the group discussions would be sent out via email for approval in a couple of days.

Minimal editing upon request was also possible if they wished to. They were also offered the option to have something of what they would say redacted: second thoughts were welcomed, so everybody should feel free to raise their hand and asking a reshot of a question,- and to change their name and face on camera, if they preferred to stay anonymous or use pseudonyms, courtesy of powerful software and AI technologies.

As far as her appearance and the name for the recordings were concerned, she chose to be called Rosalind. She preferred to appear on screen with a prettier nose, and a pair of big white sunglasses that would make an interesting disguise, just for fun more than for any real privacy concerns.

What privacy would ever save her career now, after what happened to her enviable job? She tried not to think to her unemployment status and concentrate on the tasks in front of her.

5

The individual personal interviews lasted about 90 minutes during which Rose sipped lot of water, being her lack of saliva quite severe on the day.

The group discussion went on for another hour, and was also on camera. They had to stop the recordings twice because a lady with a buffalo hump (very likely, cushing syndrome) and a man with a prosthetic leg needed the toilet.

After lunch they had to watch excerpts from the 2001 documentary Marion had mentioned to her for which they were required to note down their views and fill in a form with lots of Likert scale statements and questions. Then there was another plenary sessionin which the two groups, patients and medics, were required to discuss problems of uncertainty and decision making. Rose found it very informative and engaging.

Indeed Marion was right, the day turned out to be interesting for her at a personal level. She did not know, for instance that she was not the only one who frequently needed to rely on antibiotics in a flareup: apparently, it was quite common for people with autoimmune diseases to struggle with recurrent infections very stupid at first, like those on the skin of fingers, but for not healing easily, and often becoming a source of major complications. A doctor said that taking antibiotics was an empirical "*solution to an unknown problem*" recently judged convenient by the famous immunologist Polly Matzinger (3) who, in respect of Borrelia burgdorferi infection, noted that once it was discovered that such disease was not juvenile rheumatoid arthritis but Lyme disease, "the treatment changed from immune suppressants to antibiotics" concluding that "If a patient does better while taking antibiotics and worse without them, they should be allowed to continue to take them" (3).

Rose agreed, absolutely., and she was not the only one in the group of patients. On the other side, a young doctor argued that although very little certainty existed about possible drug-induced autoimmune diseases there was enough evidence to consider that many drugs could exacerbate   SLE symptoms, and   trigger drug allergies, and these included - hear hear! - penicillin (4).

It was not in her experience, she would have liked to have a debate on the point, but Rose did not want to contradict anybody, fight any idea, lose herself in any flow. She just wanted to recover and stay well. She needed to find a new job. She added that perhaps we all, as patients, are the main source of uncertainty, because everybody's disease is different, with or without Lupus, and we all have reactions to drugs completely different. On that, everybody else agreed.

6

The next weekend, as soon as she saw her in the changing room of the swimming pool, Marion said to Rose: "The producer asked me to contact you and see if you would be available to another focus group in case he needed it. Apparently the director is not convinced with the script, he wants more research done, and more contents, possibly more in depth conversations with some of the patients group. So I had to tell him that I know you personally and you may be not available, as you are looking for a job, you worked as a as game designer for many years, that probably you may be also interested in writing scripts for us, but... I wasn't sure you would accept another survey job... Oh my God Rose, you really impressed them, I am so excited for you, shall we celebrate?".

"And what did you say?"

"I said I would see you this weekend and talk to you and see if you have any further idea you want to share with us."

Rose smiled: "Alright, good. Let's go swimming and think about work on Monday then".

7

On Monday, Rose surprised herself drawing sketches on the margins of a magazine in an almost empty old pub turned into coffee shop. She started going there in the morning to avoid the depressive smell of cabbage coming into her flat from the old lady living on the ground floor. It wasn't like going to the office, but at least there was some movement of working people around her.

Those lines and symbols carried plenty of meaning to her, and ideas for action, she found worth keeping, together with the realisation she should restart writing and drawing, after a long season of harassment and then unemployment.

Embarrassed for being stared contentiously from behind the counter, after she put the magazine in her backpack, she offered to pay for it. Never mind, shrugged the waiter, or manager / owner of the place.

Rose texted Marion if she could phone her back, as she had an idea she would like to discuss: would the Director find it interesting? What if Health Documentaries Ltd commissioned her a video game script on the use of antibiotics and the hygiene hypothesis in autoimmune diseases? She would be happy to work as a freelance for the project. She was confident she could turn any documentary in something that would be appealing for a wider audience, through a video game. She would not say too much for the time being but it was clear she would kill an arrogant character resembling Brian Morris, a big Pharma executive who thought he would easily survive a cholera pandemic in Yemen, thanks to an early vaccination, access to antibiotics, and clean water.

Instead he would be grotesquely killed by a deadly virus he caught while trying to rape a colleague in the cloakroom of their London's headquarter, few weeks earlier.

"Marion, beware that any personal reference is accidental. (emoticon emoticon)" she added.

Her friend texted back straightaway: "You bloody game freak. it's a genius idea, come for lunch and tell me more".

Notes

(1) The hygiene hypothesis was first formulated in the 1980s to try to explain allergies. It then evolved into saying that excessive banishing of bacteria and germs from our lives, particularly in childhood, makes the body prone to develop autoimmune diseases.

Among the recent reviews on the subjects, that trace back the origin of the hypothesis and connects with the most recent studies from epidemiology, immunology, microbiology and anthropology, see: Pfefferle PI et al, *The Hygiene Hypothesis – Learning From but Not Living in the Past*, Front. Immunol. 2021, 12:635935; and Bach J-F, *Revisiting the Hygiene Hypothesis in the Context of Autoimmunity*, Front. Immunol, 2021, 11:615192.

(2) "Body Wars" is a 2001 documentary written and directed by Glenn Krawczyk and produced by Natural History NZ Ltd. The film covered the so called hygiene hypothesis in the aetiology of autoimmune diseases as it was formulated by studies in the 1980s and 1990s. It also quoted several clinical cases that seemed to support the hypothesis, matching the metaphor more than a thoroughly convincing theoretical framework endorsed by immunologists and epidemiologists, that people with autoimmune diseases needed to *"restore peace with bodies at war with themselves"*. One of the most convincing arguments to research the hygiene hypothesis at the time was provided by NASA in that: astronauts in space, eating radiated sterile foods and living in sterile spaces, allegedly become immunocompromised. In the following years the hygiene hypothesis became in itself dangerous for people to endorse without medical supervision: in fact, exposure to pathogens for people immunocompromised or who had already shown autoimmunity issues, as well as the avoidance or withdrawal of antibiotics due to general public health policies addressing antimicrobial resistance, could be catastrophic, leading for some individuals straight into sepsi and other serious life complications.

The hygiene hypothesis has nonetheless become popular over the last two decades without losing attractiveness for scientists because of the increasing convergence of interests from several disciplines to understand more about the impact of the gut microbiome on the immune system. It has contributed to more general understanding of the role of bacteria in human health and disease, and the growing importance of seeing human health in connection with environmental issues. On one side it seems clear to some scientists that viral or "fictitious" bacterial infections treated with antibiotics have made more harm than good over the last century and increased the problems of antibiotics resistance. Abuses of penicillin in particular are considered the main enemy of the healthy immune system in the hygiene hypothesis. Many bacteria, for instance strains of e.coli, are indeed very helpful for our gut health whilst only one strain of e.coli is dangerous. On the other side there are scientists who point to the extraordinary historical and current evidence that people have been surviving to deadly infections, including tuberculosis, Lyme and other chronic disease caused by bacteria precisely because of the availability of large spectrum antibiotics, used also as a prophylactic solution, without knowing precisely what type of parasite has caused a certain infection in the first place.

(3) Matzinger P, *Autoimmunity: Are we asking the right question?* Front. Immunol., 2022, 13:864633.

(4) Hogan, JJ et al, *Drug-Induced Glomerular Disease: Immune-Mediated Injury*, Clin J Am Soc Nephrol, 2015, 10: 1300–1310.

Teeth of Love

"Did they tell you at any time your dental abscess could be a sign of a more systemic problem, such as sarcoidosis or... what is called?"

"Sjögren's, Sjögren's disease"

"Yes, Sjögren's disease?" (1)

"No, never heard of sarcoidosis so far...". Amina smiled, showing her fingers crossed to the therapist. "The diagnosis of Sjögren's was very further down the line. But I got periodontitis twenty or so years ago, plus other early signs...".

"So, why did you need hospitalisation, do you remember what was the reason of that unusual treatment, for a tooth extraction?"

"No, not really". Amina seemed confused. Or she just needed a pause, and to drink some water.

Ms Fowler paused too. "I need the bathroom" she lied, to give her client more time.

Ms Fowler did not think this confident lady needed cognitive behavioural therapy, actually: Amina had come to her for an assessment via a weird chain of referrals from a GP, then a dentist, then she was seen at the hospital dental clinic, but referred back to a rheumatology department, than to ophthalmology, than she refused to be seen by an ocular plastic surgeon as she did not want to talk about any aesthetic surgery for her eyes at the moment. She had gone through lot of stress, accumulating evidence of a very dysfunctional immune system over the last twenty years, with co-morbidities multiplying year after year.

Amina's latest diagnosis was of suspected Myasthenia Gravis as a possible degeneration of Thyroid Eye Disease (Graves' orbitopathy) in the context of Sjögren's. In a nutshell, and on top of lots of dietary and musculoskeletal requirements and routines, she needed to be reassured that her protruded and misaligned eyes, with an intermittent squint, could be perfectly acceptable socially, if she first started to consider it as such.

Everything was uncertain and complicated in her case: the lack of care was the other side of a lack of cure, nobody was really responsible for. All in all she was doing well with self-care and management of the symptoms.

Amina's slightly deformed face appearance, with a cheek and an eyelid drooping, did not facilitate interacting with people as she was used to, and that was undeniable. But she had excellent communication skills, she was very good at managing her disease, eyes and sight in particular, so she shouldn't fear at all any embarrassment in others.

She could wear sunglasses and smile anytime she really wanted or needed to hide her misaligned eyes. It was in her absolute right to not consider a surgical operation that very likely would not resolve the issue in the long term. She should just assume that everybody would liaise with her exactly as they were used to.

In spite of her auspicious thoughts about the patient, when she came back to her chair, in her cozy studio, Ms Fowler saw Amina with the same expression of great sadness, smiling but with immense melancholy. She did not seem keen to remember those years of a very difficult adolescence in which she started having symptoms of rheumatic disease and frequent infections, but the therapist thought it might be helpful if she remembered her own story of resilience in dealing with her own health problems since that young age.

"So, we were talking about that operation Amina..." Ms Fowler was ready to drill again. "All teenagers experience some degree of dental decay, dental problems are very common in puberty but an operation in total anaesthesia for a tooth extraction...come on, it must have been something very unusual, terrifying too...".

"Yes, the abscess covered the whole left side of my face and neck... it was because of a tooth infection... and yes, the pain was unbearable... I remember my mum had the idea it would go away on its own, and then also the antibiotics did not work, so... the abscess just became bigger and bigger. Then the dentist said to my mother it wasn't something he could deal with in his walking-in studio, because the antibiotic had not worked. The abscess needed to be drained in a hospital setting... but she disagreed, she could not really understand".

"And it was very painful for you...".

"It was unbearable. Not just that. My face was like in that film, Elephant Man, I do not know if you have ever seen it... totally deform.".

"Oh dear, and what was your mother reaction to that?"

"She seemed not to see me, literally. Also, I think my mum did not trust the NHS dentist at all at that time... she delayed the tooth extraction, she even tried to oppose the operation... she could not understand why for a simple molar extraction I needed an urgent surgical operation under total anaesthesia at the hospital. But the more the intervention was delayed, the bigger and more painful the abscess became...".

"And what did they say to you at school? Wasn't any teacher or classmate able to help?"

"I cannot remember any moment at school with that   facial disfiguration... you know... a massive abscess extending to my left cheek and neck... I think nobody wanted to look at me... I cannot remember exactly what happened but I think I stayed away from school for at least one month..."

"But eventually your mum was convinced by the dentist...".

"Yes, she was. I was accepted by a dental clinic where all the nurses were nuns and somehow she trusted that idea. It wasn't a proper private hospital, that we could not afford... perhaps the dentist found a way to have the operation done by the NHS but in a private clinic for some reasons... I do not know... I had to stay there for one week or so after the intervention, and receive antibiotics intravenously... The infection had not resolved with normal antibiotics and the abscess needed surgical drainage. But that explanation did not mean anything to me... You know... at 14, when all my posh classmates were talking about going out, dancing, dressing up, make up, shoes and so on, I was experiencing the shame of the sheer poverty of my family, with my autistic mother having those mental crisis, headaches and hallucinations and the like, plus a sudden monstrous appearance... it was too much, too hard, incredibly hard. I do not think I ever felt again a similar sense of devastation from the inside of me, but I wanted to return to go to school as soon as possible".

"What was that sensation of devastation from the inside?"

"I guess the dentist was afraid that I could develop sepsis, or I had already developed sepsis, and that was the rationale of the hospitalisation. I understood that.   But my age and my mother's agitation might have contributed to make everything very difficult at another level, I mean they might have decided the operation in order to prevent further complications with my mum unable to proper accept the fact I needed intravenous antibiotics, not easy to deal with at home.... So... I do not know, I just felt something was mounting up from the inside of me somewhere, because I had no power, no agency on my own health, and it was reaching into my mind too... I remember I started talking awry, for instance, swearing at my teachers, at the neighbours... but it wasn't really me shouting all those words... I think some social pressure on my mother started at that point, that I needed to sort out the abscess as soon as possible.... I remember one of her colleagues stopping by our garage to say to her that she was the most selfish mother she had ever known...a sticky judgement, that perhaps she never really understood... On the contrary, she felt she was the one who was suffering, you know... she was the one who needed support and assistance... But somehow, she got it. "

Amina exhaled, that was a very fatigued memory. She sipped some water.

Ms Fowler smiled all her sympathy and encouragement. Amina should see the positive side of looking back: "Well done, Amina, I think it was very clever of you actually... you were shouting you needed help at that point, and it worked, you got the help you needed, you could have died of sepsi without that operation". Then she asked if Amina had ever thought that her dramatic teenager tooth extraction with total anaesthesia was a warning of something wrong with her immune system, a signal of something that would come out many years later.

"No, not really, it was only much later on, after the frequent episodes of gum inflammation, the periodontitis, the several extractions of teeth after other explosive granulomas under the roots of the teeth that I had a genetic and microbiological analysis of my mouth bacteria. It was a revelation. But by then... I was already over 40 years old. The genetic analysis showed that I am prone to have a small percentage of very dangerous bacteria that are also associated with arthralgia symptoms and rheumatic conditions. It's not unusual, the dentist explained, that people with serious inflammation, gingivitis or periodontitis develop autoimmune diseases, diagnosed later in life... Treating the gums with laser therapy was really helpful (2). Also, to get rid of those bacteria, more frequent than usual hygiene sessions are highly recommended.

Composite restoration made the extreme sensitiveness to cold and heat of my enamel and gums gradually becoming more bearable... Few implants and good crowns saved my smile as much as possible, as well as my mastication... In sum, I have always been lot of work for the dentists, haven't I?" Amina smiled.

"All in all, do you still feel your mum was responsible for all that sufferance, your abscesses, the teeth operation, your appearance... in those circumstances?"

"Well, responsible perhaps is not the right word. My mother grew up in Africa, you know... her family owned a plantation before they came to England... they did not have any dentist for a long time as far as I can remember from family tales... perhaps at some point they had somebody working as a dentist in the village, but... I am not sure about the credentials of those doctors either... She grew up with an idiosyncratic relationship with dentists. I remember her saying to me in many occasions, kind of very scared, not to go to the dentist, not to spend money for dentist care, and not to trust dentists' advice for extractions.   *Don't let them take out your teeth* she often shouted at me when I told her I had toothache and I was about to go to the dentist. She delayed her own dental care up to the point she lost all of her own teeth, and suffered unbearable pain, while both me and my younger brother were desperately trying to convince her she needed to go to the dentist, and very urgently. There is no worse deaf of somebody who does not want to hear. But eventually we made it somehow... she went to the dentist when she was already over 70s... it was discovered then she had many broken teeth, decayed and rotten teeth roots left behind, a disaster in her mouth... So she must have suffered a lot because of that fear of dentistry... It was also difficult for her to adapt to the dentures she was given.... The madness is that, in truth, she was not an ignorant, illiterate person, you know... she was even keen on learning about medicine, scientific issues and the like... I cannot say she did not understand what the problem was or could be, rationally, with my teeth. She did not hesitate to spend thousands of pounds to make sure my brothers had both regular dental check-ups, hygiene sessions, fillings, crowns, for instance. So it was just with me that her autistic attitude, her fears, her irrational mind would find a way to prevail and distort her judgement and decisions. It was like she could understand the importance of going to the dentist for everybody else on earth but not for the two of us... she was convinced that dentists would not do any good to the two of us.... she kind of projected on me and on my teeth, and dental health, her own fear of the dentist. Many years later she told me that when I was little we lived in symbiosis... Oh, well... I said that perhaps that was the reason why I couldn't wait to go and live on my own, and have the freedom to go to the dentist too!"

Ms Fowler laughed. Amina seemed much more relaxed and laughed too. It was clearly a relief for her to talk openly about her autistic, difficult and yet much loved mother.

"Luckily your dentist insisted and you had that operation Amina...".

"Yes. I remember my rage when I woke up from the anaesthesia, in that hospital bed, surrounded by nuns withdrawing water.... I shouted insults, I swore at them. I felt I was still suffering the usual awful pain, my jaw was still terribly aching. It was there that I might have had a minimal but lasting jaw dislocation".

"I see you have been diagnosed with temporomandibular jaw disorder too, you do not miss a thing" Ms Fowler pushed on her lighthearted tone, as she would recommend Amina to continue to be in control of her complex health problems.

"Yes", Amina smiled too. "Also this was recognised only later on.... After the abscess receded, the pain was still strong in my face and neck... the tooth had been extracted, the abscess had been drained, but it took few days for the face to go back to a normal shape and the pain to disappear... I remember fear and desperation. I thought the abscess had left scars in my jaw that would never heal... Everything was aching in my body, not just the neck, I could not even speak but in a sort of eruptive, furious way, with explosions of insults... I was in pain, physically and mentally... in retrospect that might have been a juvenile anticipation of the dry mouth I suffer now... but in those days nobody thought I should be tested for diseases there were actually still unknown....well perhaps already known but only in science labs, you know... back in the 1970s and 1980s, not by family doctors nor by dentists..." (3)

Amina took a sip of water, than she continued with a raft of memories: "Plus, I remember my mother's disappointment when she came to see me at the clinic and learned I should stay in the hospital for transfusions and intravenous antibiotics for a week... and I had insulted the nuns. It seemed she blamed me, that it was my fault if I was not only prone to have severe dental problems at such a young age, but also needed to stay hospitalised after the removal of an infected molar. In the end, everything was fine: we laughed at the insults I had shouted to the nuns after the anaesthesia, but she was a very difficult mother to care for and deal with at that young age, with pretty much no independence."

"However it was not just your mother's fear of dentists to create the problems you had, wasn't it?" Ms Fowler said, turning in direction of the cause for her numerous health problems and feelings, rooted into the dysfunction of her immune system. "I see here you reported that you continued to have abscesses rapidly developing out of the blue later on.... Between the age of thirteen and your early thirties you lost or you required fillings for all of your molars and premolars, that is quite unusual...".

"Yes, it was only after I started work at 19 that I could eventually pay for my own regular dental check-ups and treatments. My mouth was still plagued with recurrent infections but I was able to take control of it, to replace all the cheap fillings with safer and better crowns in my 20s and early 30s. I had the money to do it. Later on I made loans so I could be able to pay for periodontal treatment, for implants, for the frequent hygiene sessions, you know... dental costs were and still are a massive expense, almost impossible to afford if you have low or no income... I was lucky that for a couple of decades I was able to pay for private dental treatments without problems, as I was earning a good salary, and that put a halt to an avalanche of dental issues I had been suffering since childhood...   Perhaps the single one thing that improved my quality of life and prevented further abscesses was to give up some foods upon suggestion of dentists that witnessed my progressive gum inflammation and blisters, and gave me very good advice.... Also giving up cigarettes smoking was the decisive good thing to do in my 40s... With the elimination of gluten I have almost got rid of any further gum swelling, and also mouth ulcers became rarer.... in sum, it seems unbelievable now when I think about it but it took more than 50 years to understand that I have lot of autoimmunity issues, the non celiac gluten sensitivity, etcetera etcetera... these created lot of dental problems as well, year after year... Aging does not help at all with anything in autoimmunity either. Perhaps I could have also prevented the massive periodontitis in my 40s if I only had been tested for these food intolerances in those years, if I had done the genetic testing for the bacteria earlier on..."

"What would you say was the ultimate origin of your dental issues then? Food intolerances? Or autoimmunity?"

"Love. I would say teeth need love..."

Ms Fowler laughed. "You see Amina, you are so intelligent, you already know if you love yourself unconditionally, you can deal with untreatable problems from the inside as well as from the outside of you".

"Yes, I can" Amina smiled too.

Notes

(1) About 75% of the adult population develop some sort of periodontal disease in their life. This happens for a wide range of reasons, including poor dental hygiene, but also because of a genetic propensity to have colonies of nasty bacteria harbouring in the gum and attacking the tissue integrity, causing chronic inflammation, blisters, bouts of infections. Gum disease can therefore be seen as one of the numerous non specific symptoms of Sjögren's but for the fact that the incidence and severity of periodontitis, loss of teeth and abscesses are worse for these patients than for the rest of the population. At the core of dental problems for Sjögren's patients is also the reduced or intermittent secretion of saliva that accelerate processes of decay, gum inflammation, ulcers and periodontal disease. A recent review by Yang B et al (*The association of periodontal diseases and Sjögren's syndrome: A systematic review and meta-analysis,* Front Med, 2023 Jan 5;9:904638), based on an impressive meta-analysis of 21 worldwide studies involving 11435 patients, clarified the complex correlation between periodontitis and Sjögren's. Many experts and scholars - particularly in the realm of rheumatology - still in 2025 believe there is no need to recommend early intervention and frequent dental check ups to Sjögren's patients compared to the normal population. For an overview of the problems see also: Vujovic, S. et al., *Oral Health and Oral Health-Related Quality of Life in Patients with Primary Sjögren's Syndrome,* Medicina, 2023, 59, 473.

(2) The most common autoimmune diseases associated with periodontal disease are rheumatoid arthritis, systemic lupus erythematosus, Sjögren's, thrombocytopenia purpura. Several dental

clinics now offer treatment of periodontal disease with lasertherapy and / or   with other technologies of light. See for instance: *Low level laser therapy in the treatment of periodontal diseas*, Laser Therapy, 16, 4: 199-206; *Innovative approach to oral health in Sjögren's syndrome*, Dentistry IQ, March 6, 2025.

(3)   MacFarlane, TW and Mason, DK, *Changes in the oral flora in Sjögren's syndrome*, J. clin. Path., 1974, 27, 416-419.

Postface

In 2022 I started a research and writing project about autoimmune diseases and knowledge management, "The Sicca Messenger", the purpose of which was to investigate aspects of health literacy, research, clinical guidance, public policies. I would look into these complex matters from the perspective, necessarily holistic, of the informed patient, and write my reflections for improvements, using all the notes on my scale.

Having done similar exercises for almost four decades in different subject areas and industries, I was confident I could write everything I had to say in an essay, and in plain English.

I was soon confronted with the finiteness of the non-fiction world, with the challenge of integrating not only different bodies of knowledge, insight from different disciplines, medical protocols, educational curricula and standards of care established during different historical periods, but also the subjective understanding of these conditions within patients associations, communities of practice, pharmaceutical companies, social media and my own subjective knowledge

Looking at such complex picture, one subject became a prominent landmark, claiming attention and suggesting fiction as a potentially better genre compared to non-fiction in order to accomplish at least part of my mission: adverse childhood experiences in the aetiology of autoimmune diseases, and particularly in systemic autoimmune diseases, in which autoimmunity affects the entire body, like in Sjögren's or Lupus.

As of 2025 there is compelling consensus and scientific evidence worldwide that we are born with some innate, polygenic predisposition to autoimmune diseases, also called genetic susceptibility, but we actually develop an active disease only if we go through highly variable, subjective experiences of injury, loss, trauma, abuse, damage to the body and the mind.

In a nutshell, the accidents we survive in our life may, hopefully and with time, fade away but their legacy is likely to remain as an indelible mark on our immune system, causing lasting damage, permanent impairments, chronic diseases, particularly if they occur in childhood, affecting the development of the immune mind and body.

Over the last thirty years, starting with a pivotal study published in 1979 about the findings on children who had been buried alive (1), academic disciplines have proved that adverse childhood experiences increase the probability of cellular and metabolic damages, with lasting consequences for the immune system.

A retrospective cohort study published in 2009 with data of over 15000 adults investigated the risks of developing autoimmune diseases for people who had adverse childhood experiences (ACEs). These were defined as childhood physical, emotional or sexual abuse, witnessing domestic violence, growing up with household substance abuse, mental illness, parental divorce and / or with an incarcerated household member. The findings were impressive: "sixty-four percent reported at least one ACE and persons with two or more ACEs were at a 70% increased risk for hospitalisation with immunopathologies" (2).

More recently, UK Biobank data related to 108,915 women (3) provided convincing evidence of "associations between common adverse childhood experiences and a higher prevalence of several specific autoimmune diseases among adult women", namely Thyroid disease, Sjögren's disease, rheumatoid arthritis, Systemic Lupus Erythematosus, psoriasis, and polymyalgia rheumatica.

These data validated opinions and hypothesis discussed by patients and medics since long.

The literature about adverse childhood experiences that I consulted convinced me that whatever health public policy initiative or health literacy programme in this area should start with prevention: better care for children, better parenting, better family planning, and, ideally, the total eradication of childhood food poverty and trauma (4).

Adverse childhood experiences could be seen as a lasting sign of "diathesis" (a medical term for vulnerability or predisposition) that makes some individuals more likely to be penalised in life by harmful stressors, compared to those who do not experience such burden earlier in life.

It is quite hard to predict who among these two broad categories of people, the resilient and the vulnerable, are going to suffer later in life from autoimmunity, or from flashbacks and psychosis. It is also impossible to predict when and how, in a lifetime the expectation of which is now spanning almost a century, adverse childhood experiences would put somebody in the resilient or in the vulnerable category, or halfway through the two, like myself, like many of the characters protagonists in the stories of *The Blind Spot*.

In each story, I tried to offer multiple narrative layers the reader can engage with. Interwoven narratives are a fascinating challenge for any writer: who wouldn't like to be able to write like Umberto Eco does in "Il nome della Rosa"? But more than a literary ambition, what drove me to the actual format of these short stories is the fact that I wanted to write about adverse childhood experiences and autoimmune diseases integrating the perception, ignorance of disease or subjective knowledge of the patient with factual information, medical research and clinical guidelines publicly available. I wanted the text to be engaging and interesting for the student, the young doctor, the carer, and of course for the patient wanting to learn something insightful and reassuring, in spite of the enormous uncertainty, and vagueness of public knowledge.

In fact, this is an area of medical research in which, on a daily basis, we listen to announcements of fascinating discoveries, powered by artificial intelligence, and we cannot really make up our minds on what is true and what is aspirational or experimental: immunology and molecular medicine are revolutionising the way we look at health and diseases, but how many wrong pathways will be taken to come to real innovation for health and longevity in our lifespan?

Immunology is a discipline with great gaps in knowledge, in spite of the empirical uncontroverted evidence that vaccines save lives: as of 2025 we still do not know how many types of cells make the immune system (the Human Cell Atlas project is fasting getting there).

I return on problems of knowledge and research in *The Sicca Messenger* essay. Here, starting from *The Burn,* in which multiple perspectives intersect the weaved fabric of the story presented through a diary, I aimed at rendering the complexity of growing up and then living with incurable diseases that often affect several members of the same family, either because of inborn errors of immunity (like Down Syndrome) or because of autoimmune diseases (like rheumatoid arthritis), left undetected or undiagnosed for many years.

Also in *The surgeon with the parakeets and the lost appendix*, *The patch*, *Teeth of Love*, in spite of such overwhelming uncertainty about treatments, I wanted to convey the need to preserve our trust in medicine. At the same time I needed to reflect the positivity of deeply personal journeys into the matters, that leverage on self-care and personal experimentation more than conventional protocols and methods, far away from conspiracy theories, and always looking critically to case-histories or experts' advice, landing on an ephemeral balance of mindfulness as the only actual way of living with chronic disease and enjoying our longevity. In this mix, I believe, is where understanding of adverse childhood experiences (not less than traumas and injuries in adulthood) can bring empowering suggestions to build resilience and tolerance, to lower inflammation, to ask for personalised care.

I am among those who believe that subjective knowledge represents a valuable contribution to the collective understanding of autoimmune diseases. It is a different type of knowledge, not obtainable directly through scientific methods and processes, nor through spiritual practices. Self-care insight, self-reflective judgements are nonetheless increasingly recognised as a potentially very valid type of contributions to good outcomes in clinical practices, particularly in lifestyle and functional medicine. Molecular and biomedical studies are bringing more evidence on how complex and unique is the behaviour of the immune system for each human being, revealing that what has been labelled and dismissed as "anecdotical" over the last two centuries may actually bring some qualitative insight, very helpful to clinical practice and personalised medicine as well as to research along sustainable, ethical, non harmful pathways.

We are also becoming more aware of the challenge of science communication.

The complexity of diagnosis and acceptance of autoimmune diseases is evident, I hope, in some stories (*The Blind Spot*, *The missed abortion*, *The sun's kisses*, *The Lazy eye*, *Two gory twins*, *Sinéad and the sound of my heart*) in which the protagonists are confronted with the emotional toll of disease on their cognitive and emotional lives. The fascination for a social dimension of knowledge very often leaves these characters with frustration: they assume there are answers to be found, but they are often left with more unanswered questions. Nonetheless, they choose to prioritise self-care against the escalation or perpetuation of fights or flights responses, nor they want to follow thoughts that would pull them into downward spirals of depression, apathy, fatigue.

The same is true for the characters of the other stories, with different nuances always tinted with some optimism. The spark of trust in our sentient nature, in our ability to subjective and objective critical knowledge, could be found particularly in between the lines of *Penicillin power*, *Schirmer's test for a man*, *The phantom tonsils*, *A casual lymph*, *Teeth of love* where the protagonists have really touched the limits of their tolerance to stress and impairments caused by autoimmunity: yet, they do want to get on with their lives, with the adjustments they need, no matter the conditions they have developed.

Each story contains something from my own lived experience and biography in various proportions. Although very much inspired by this, all the stories in *"The Blind Spot"* are works of fiction, "hybridised" with nonfiction insertions for the purpose of sharing reliable scientific information and references to medical studies.

I wish the reader can find in any of the stories of *The Blind Spot* something to learn, a factual content, an idea to improve the quality of life, intertwined with entertaining characters and contexts.

The narrative fabric offers a perspective on the aetiology and the development of autoimmune diseases: this may continue to puzzle patients, doctors and researchers for a long time. Conversely, our days are numbered: we should make the most of them, in spite of our individual and collective blind spots.

Notes

(1) Terr, L., *The Children of Chowchilla*, "The Psychoanalytic Study of the Child, 34 (1979), 547-623.

(2) Dube, S. et al., *Cumulative Childhood Stress and Autoimmune Diseases in Adults*, Psycosomatic medicine, (71), February-March 2009, Issue 2.

(3) Köhler-Forsberg, O. et al., *Adverse childhood experiences, mental distress, and autoimmune disease in adult women: findings from two large cohort studies*, Psychological Medicine, 2025 (55), e36, 1–10.

(4) Osofsky, SD and McAlister Goves, B (eds), *Violence and trauma in the lives of children*, Praeger, 2018.

About the Author

Brunella Longo, Technologist and Writer, has pioneered many innovations in information science and information management, sharing original ideas and lessons learned through project documentation, technical papers, books, articles, training and e-learning courses, before writing fiction and nonfiction books on autoimmune diseases and knowledge management, including "Source. Poems about homelessness", "The Blind Spot" and "The Sicca Messenger" (2025).

Her other recent titles include "Book Publishing and the Internet" (2023), the pamphlet "The end of freedom (to write what you want): A short trip into the world of online influence powered by AI and crip autotheory" (2025), "Knowledge Changes", a collection of article previously published as "icm2re (I Changed My Mind Reviewing Everything)" on data, knowledge and change management (2012-2022).